JOACHIM MASANNEK

The Wild Soccer Bunch

Translated from the German by Helga Schier

Editor: Michael Part

Original title: Leon, der Slalomdribbler
©2002 Baumhaus Verlag GmbH, Frankfurt am Main, Germany
Die Wilden Fussballkerle™ Joachim Masannek & Jan Birck

Special thanks to:
Daniel Klein
Yaron, Yonatan and Guy Ginsberg.

Library of Congress Cataloging-in-Publication data available.

ISBN 978-0-9844257-0-9

Published by Sole Books

First Edition May 2010
Printed in the United States of America

Layout: Lynn M. Snyder

10987654321

566TB548, April, 2010

Hi *Wild Bunch* fans!

I am a huge fan of *The Wild Soccer Bunch!* They are a crew of zany, extraordinary, fun-loving soccer players. More important, they are great friends!

Kids everywhere ask me how they can become a professional player, like me.

Well, for starters you've really got to love this game! I've been playing soccer competitively since I was five years old. I started out playing in my neighborhood park, just like many of you. There, I learned the basics: how to dribble, pass, and of course, how to score. Most of all, I learned how to be a team player.

If I was ten years old again, I would try out for the *Wild Soccer Bunch,* and hopefully I'd make the team. I know we would play some tough opponents, win close games, and share unforgettable adventures. And we'd always be the wildest bunch of soccer players anywhere!

Your Friend and Teammate,

Landon Donovan

JOACHIM MASANNEK

The Wild Soccer Bunch

Book 1

Kevin, the Star Striker

Illustrations by Jan Birck

TABLE OF CONTENTS

The *Wild Bunch* _ _ _ _ _ _ _ _ _ _ _ _ _ _ 9

The *Wild Bunch* Doesn't Hibernate_ _ _ _ _ _ _ 15

The End of the World _ _ _ _ _ _ _ _ _ _ _ 22

Kevin's Dream _ _ _ _ _ _ _ _ _ _ _ _ _ _ 27

Tyler, the Pain! _ _ _ _ _ _ _ _ _ _ _ _ _ 32

Long Gone 'Cause Nothing Can Stop Us! _ _ _ _ 37

Trapped! _ _ _ _ _ _ _ _ _ _ _ _ _ _ _ _ 45

Never Give Up!_ _ _ _ _ _ _ _ _ _ _ _ _ _ 50

With Bated Breath _ _ _ _ _ _ _ _ _ _ _ _ 59

Larry, of Course! _ _ _ _ _ _ _ _ _ _ _ _ _ 63

Moms and Dads _ _ _ _ _ _ _ _ _ _ _ _ _ 68

The First Touch _ _ _ _ _ _ _ _ _ _ _ _ _ 80

A Moment of Truth _ _ _ _ _ _ _ _ _ _ _ _ 86

He Who Puts a Spell on the Ball _ _ _ _ _ _ 95

Mr. Invincible _ _ _ _ _ _ _ _ _ _ _ _ _ _ 100

The Best Soccer Players in the World _ _ _ _ _ 103

The Bulldozer's Surprise Attack_ _ _ _ _ _ _ 108

A Dark Night and an Even Darker Morning _ _ _ _ 117

Be Wild! _ _ _ _ _ _ _ _ _ _ _ _ _ _ _ 124

Roger the Hero! _ _ _ _ _ _ _ _ _ _ _ _ 131

Even Wilder! _ _ _ _ _ _ _ _ _ _ _ _ _ 135

The *Wild Bunch*

Hey you! Yes, I am talking to you! You made it!

I thought we'd never get to know each other. My name is Kevin, and that's us: the *Wild Bunch*. Right about now a *nice* children's book author would say we are eleven friends and a cute dog. And we love to play soccer. But I am here to tell you I am one of the *Wild Bunch* and what you are reading is not a children's book. It's real; it's as real as life. Totally! My dog Sox is not just cute, and we are not just eleven friends. We are much more: We are dangerous and we are wild. Bet your life on it.

Danny, for example, is my best friend. He is the world's fastest right forward. I totally rely on him, and I hope he'll never stop playing soccer. But Danny is interested in many other things, too. He's even interested in — you're not going to believe this — he's even interested in — *girls*.

Oh man! Not even Tyler is interested in girls yet, and he's ten already! Tyler is my big brother, by the way, and like all big brothers, he can be a pain. He drives me crazy! But what can you do? You need your brother, and that's that. Like the air you breathe. And on the field, nothing works without him. He is the brains and the heart of the *Wild Bunch* machine. For one reason: He never gives up. My brother Tyler is our number 10, and I'm very proud of that. Period.

Kyle, on the other hand, comes on the sly and without his parents' permission. His father wants him to be a golf pro or a tennis ace. But Kyle has other plans. Whenever he manages to bolt, he is in our goal. And if you ask me, he won't do much of anything else. He's a natural. He's a born goalie. In my opinion, anyone who scores a goal against Kyle will end up in the *Guinness Book of World Records*.

Ask the cannon. He's already in there. But that's all you're going to get out of him.

Alex Alexander, nicknamed the cannon, doesn't talk much. He's a man of action, and he has the strongest kick in the world. And there aren't any words to describe it. When Kyle got in front of him — he just hurled him into the net along with the ball.

That was the one time he outplayed Julian. Julian Fort Knox is our all-in-one defender. Truly, he's playing like four defenders in one player! We call him Fort Knox because this is where our country keeps the gold. No one gets into Fort Knox, and no one gets past Julian.

Now we come to Roger. Roger the hero! But he wasn't always called that. I don't want to trash talk anyone, but you tell me: Would a blind man think he could be a photographer?

Then why does Roger think he can play soccer? But I'm not allowed to say anything because Danny protects him. Maybe Danny is right. There is definitely no one like Roger. He is one-of-a-kind!

You probably think I'm mean for talking about him like this, but what can I say?

Life is mean — especially when it comes to soccer. And soccer is Diego's life, too. Diego is our tornado. He has asthma, and when he has an attack, he's just a regular left forward. But when he's on his game, he's faster than a tornado.

Or Joey. Joey is the exact opposite of Kyle, our goalie. Kyle is rich, but Joey's mother is poor and she's out of work. That's why they live in a van, which is kind of cool because they can go wherever they want, *whenever* they want.

But Joey can't afford cleats.

He doesn't even have a jacket. Sometimes he doesn't even show up. That's because his mother drinks a lot. Joey never talks about it and he tries not to show it, but you can see it in his face when he presses his lips together real hard. You just know he's in pain. But when everything is fine, Joey plays soccer like a magician and it's a wonder to watch. It's as if he put a spell on the ball.

When Joey is on, he plays even better than me: I, Kevin, the master dribbler, the Star Striker, and the quickest assist there is.

At least that's what Larry calls me, when I'm not a ball-hog or too selfish or too stubborn. Between you and me, that's exactly what I am sometimes.

Larry is our coach and he always knows best. He may only work the lemonade stand at the soccer field and maybe he didn't get very far in life — but Larry was almost a soccer pro, and to us, he will always be the greatest coach in the world.

Together, we are the *Wild Soccer Bunch,* the best soccer team in the world. And the only team I ever want to play with. But it wasn't always this way. A lot had to happen before we got our act together and the *Wild Soccer Bunch* became a team. Don't get me wrong, it's always hard starting out, but in our case, it was really hard. As hard as the ground in our neighborhood on the north side of Chicago. The ground was hard because it was frozen solid and covered in snow. The wind blew like there was no tomorrow. That's why they call it The Windy City. Winter, eternal and never-ending, ruled the day. And on top of that, Mickey, the Bulldozer, and his *Unbeatables*, got in our way.

The *Wild Bunch* Doesn't Hibernate

The year we made ourselves into a team, winter reached far into the month of April. Spring break was right at our door, and only five short days separated us from the most fantastic two weeks of a nine-year-old boy's entire year. Two weeks without school or homework. Two weeks, during which none of us would be kidnapped by our parents and whisked off to a far-away island or an isolated mountain range. In those two weeks we would run to the soccer field right after breakfast and not return until sunset. In those two weeks there would be nothing but soccer from dawn to dusk, with lemonade from Larry's stand during the breaks. Imagine it. How the lemonade quenches your thirst and soothes your parched lips. How the warm early summer wind caresses your sweaty hair. How your naked toes, freed from your cleats at last, dig into the dirt that's still too cold for comfort. Are you with me? Now imagine how you hang on Larry's every word as he tells you stories from the golden days of soccer. Days we didn't know, but days that Larry's words bring to life right before our eyes. Stories about the best players of all time who reigned over the soccer fields. He told us about Diego Maradona,

El Diez, who was a master dribbler, just like me. Or Johan Cruyff, who played total football and was second only to Pele. He told us stories about Pele, more and more stories about Pele, the best soccer player ever, and more recent stories about Mia Hamm, the best American woman soccer player of all time. But this year, winter wouldn't go away. At least seven inches of snow and ice covered the soccer field and the city, muffling our dreams.

My brother Tyler and I were sitting on the floor in our room, staring through the ice crystals on our window, up into the grey sky above Wilson Street. There were only four more days until spring break. The cleats we got for Christmas were making our feet itch. My soccer ball, scratched and scuffed, sat on my lap. We imagined we were hibernating, like the grizzlies in Canada. But we felt more like caged tigers at the Lincoln Park Zoo. My soccer ball flew back and forth, faster and faster. We knew it might get us into trouble, but we couldn't stop. At school our teachers lectured about the Ice Age. I didn't find that funny at all. I figured if people in the Ice Age had known about soccer, they wouldn't have survived. Tyler and I were no longer sitting on the floor.

We were standing up, enthusiastically throwing the ball back and forth between us, faster and faster. We called it goalie training. Problem was, Tyler was our number 10, the midfield playmaker, and I was our center forward. What's the use of goalie training? We needed some action!

So we started kicking the ball at the wall. BAM! Always alternating. BAM! BAM!

The same thing was happening at my best friend Danny's house at 44 Dearborn Street. He fired the ball at the wall of his room. BAM! So did Julian and his little

brother Josh, in the house across the street. But two blocks away, in the fancy house at One Woodlawn Avenue, Alex couldn't go into his room. That's where his little sister kept her Barbie dollhouse. No problem. He just slammed the ball against the living room wall. BAM! There was a small open space between the mirror and the china cabinet. BAM! That was his goal.

Drum rolls echoed from house to house, all the way across town. BAM! From Wilson to Dearborn to Woodlawn. BAM! Only Roger the Hero didn't participate. He was sitting at home, in his small town house at 1236 Oak Park Avenue, watching in helpless disbelief as the giggling daughters of his mother's friends put curlers in his red hair. But then he heard the drum rolls from across town. And they gave him strength and hope.

Only three more days until spring break, and the sky was still grey. Fat, fist-shaped snowflakes splashed against the window as if they wanted to smother everything underneath with a sticky glob of cotton candy. But the drum rolls grew louder. BAM! BAM! BAM! The damp snow foreshadowed the coming thaw, and that gave us strength.

Only two more days, and the sun finally came out, peeking through a tiny little crack in the stone gray sky. Our drum rolls finally fought back the winter. The last snowflakes danced in the sunlight, and with them my soccer ball danced between our feet. Tyler and I were in the heat of the game now. Our room on Wilson had long become Toyota Park, and we didn't notice that we shot down one model plane after another from the ceiling. Honest, we didn't.

Alex the cannon became the man with the world's strongest kick again. He carefully got the ball ready for his free kick on the living room carpet. Next, he assessed the distance to his opponent's wall, right next to the china cabinet.

At 44 Dearborn Street, Danny, the world's fastest midfielder, stormed through his room, right along the sideline. And in the house across the street, Julian Fort Knox, the all-in-one defender, was waiting to be attacked by his little brother, who suddenly looked a lot like David Beckham.

It was fantastic! We had won! Winter was defeated and spring break was saved. Then Danny advanced too fast. He couldn't stop in time and slammed into the bookshelf. Books and boxes came crashing down on him, and Dearborn Street shook.

Next, Tyler lifted the ball into the air. It was the perfect chip pass. I sprinted towards it and performed a "flip over bicycle kick." That's my signature move, by the way. It was the all-decisive goal. But the ball jumped off the outside rim and thundered into the lamp. The floodlights of our Toyota Park went out and we were back on Wilson Street.

Meanwhile, Julian was at David Beckham's heels. At the last moment, he straddled to prevent a goal. He straddled and glided right into his mother's legs. She had suddenly appeared at the door, dinner in hand. Dearborn Street shook a second time, and the sandwiches flew through the air, David Beckham morphed back into Josh, and the sandwiches hit him smack in the face.

Only Woodlawn Avenue was still quiet. Alex the cannon held his breath to make it even quieter. Then he sped up. He ran and thundered the ball right over his opponent's wall and in a matter of milliseconds, the ball landed directly in the corner, a tad away from the china cabinet. Alex's face broke into his famously silent grin. That was an amazing shot!

With that famously silent grin on his lips, Alex the cannon watched as the ball bounced back from the wall and went crashing straight through the living room window. Outside, the ball kept rolling, further and further, until it was stopped by his father's foot.

For it was right at that moment that Alex's father came home from work at the bank. The famously silent grin vanished from Alex's lips. It had become completely dark, and there was only one more day until spring break.

The End of the World

The night grew quiet. Quiet like the eye of a storm. Our beds were hard as cots, and our rooms were dark and grey like prison cells. None of us slept. Danny, Julian, Josh, Alex, my brother Tyler and I were all awaiting our verdicts. Even Roger, who had done nothing wrong, was holding on to his teddy bear at 1236 Oak Park Avenue, and didn't dare breathe.

It was still quiet the next morning. We got up without a word, and were not at all surprised when, in response to our good mornings, our parents stopped talking and fell absolutely silent. You have to be careful when you're in the eye of a storm. You don't want to move, because the storm rages all around you. We all knew that. That's why we didn't even bat an eye when our moms and dads read us our sentences.

Danny, my best friend, nine years old, from 44 Dearborn, was grounded for three whole days. His ball was spirited away to the top of the highest living room shelf, where his mother's expensive china could watch over it.

Josh and Julian, six and nine years old, from the house across the street, were banned from soccer for two days.

To enforce the sentence, their mother let the air out of their soccer ball and hid the pump.

Tyler and I, ten and nine years old, from Wilson Street, were condemned to slaughter our piggy bank and pay for the lamp in our room.

But when my dad got up from the breakfast table to go to our room and take away my ball, I jumped up. I forgot all about the eye of the storm. "That's my ball!" I yelled and ran towards my room. I pushed my dad aside, zipped past him through the door, and made it into my room first. I grabbed my ball. My dad stood in the doorway, speechless. I stared at him with fury. Then I opened our hamster cage, shoved the ball inside, and locked the cage with my bicycle lock. I angrily gave the key to my dad.

"Here! Take it!" I spat with venom in his direction. "You got what you wanted!"

My dad looked at me like I was crazy. Then he took the key and left my room, shaking his head. He always said kids don't come with instruction manuals and this was one of those puzzling moments. Speaking of moments, at that precise moment, Tyler stormed in. "Are you nuts?" he yelled at me. "At least, all he ever does is lock the ball in his study, and tomorrow, when the cleaning lady comes, we'll get it out."

"That's exactly why I didn't let him take it, dude," I answered, "the cleaning lady isn't coming tomorrow."

"Oh yeah? Brilliant! One problem: you locked it up and gave him the key. So how exactly were you planning on getting the ball out of the cage?"

Tyler was really furious with me, and I was really miffed right back at him.

"It's my ball," I spat, "not yours. I can do whatever I want with it."

"Well, I guess you want it locked up forever!" Tyler responded dryly. I shoved my hands in my pocket, sheepishly. I had a plan. I always have a plan.

"Locked up forever, huh? Is that your final answer?" I could hardly conceal my grin. "Oh, I almost forgot. Did I mention I have a spare key?"

Slowly I pulled the key from my pockets.

"Tight!" Tyler said, as a huge grin spread across his face.

That same grin, however, disappeared forever from Alex the cannon's face. "Grounded for ten days with a complete soccer ban," was his sentence. Alex watched stone-faced through the fancy living room window at One Woodlawn Avenue as his father lugged three garbage bags through the gate and to the street. The bags were filled with his soccer gear. It took him over five years to save up for that equipment. And now it was going to be tossed into the back of a garbage truck that sat rumbling at the curb.

"It's not fair!" The words pounded in Alex's head as he absentmindedly played with the globe that rested on the small sideboard next to the window. "It's just not fair. *No one* can live without soccer. No one in the world. The whole round world..."

Then something amazing happened. That famously

silent grin formed on Alex's face. He tapped the globe once and watched it turn over ever so smoothly. After that, things happened very quickly. The screws that held the globe in place on the stand were a piece of cake. And in a heartbeat, the equator landed on the hardwood floor and the North Pole received a powerful kick. Alex fired the globe against the living room wall, over and over again. "Complete soccer ban? I don't think so!" he thought, and with his knee he lifted the ball up into the air until it almost kissed the ceiling. "And now a bicycle kick!" And then his thoughts became reality. Alex jumped up, gathered momentum with his left leg and mercilessly followed with his right. With a resounding thud, his foot hit the coast of Madagascar. The globe shot towards the wall like a cannon ball, bounced back, and flew through the only surviving living room window with an explosion of glass! Meanwhile, outside at the gate, Alex's father was watching the garbage truck drive off with his son's soccer gear, when the globe came crashing through the window. Alarmed, his father spun around and saw the earth as he had never seen it before, just before it hit him in the head. Alex's father was stunned. He traced the earth's trajectory, and there was his son standing framed in the shattered window, equally stunned.

"That's ten more days," he said between his teeth with a quivering voice. Alex could only numbly nod, and watch as his father picked up the globe, threw it up in the air and catapulted it into the sky with a shot that impressed even his son. "Ten plus ten, that's twenty. You're grounded for twenty days. Is that clear?" His father's words cut as sharply and deeply as those knives of glass that lay shattered on the front lawn.

But Alex did not hear those words. His mind was in the clouds as he watched the globe climb into the morning sky to meet it, higher and higher, then descend past the rising sun, down down, faster and faster, hitting the ground in the neighbor's driveway, cracking and bouncing one last time before coming to rest on the neighbor's flower bed, broken in half. Bummer! This really was the end of the world.

Kevin's Dream

The day that followed that fateful morning was sad and dreary. On our way to school, the sun disappeared behind clouds that hung low and seemed to sit on the rooftops of our neighborhood, so grey that all color was drained from them. The world was in black and white. At school, all the other kids were laughing and happily telling the teachers their plans for spring break. But that didn't bring the color back. When the teachers asked us what we were going to do, we had nothing to tell. We were silent. We were silent for Alex, who was grounded for twenty days. We were silent for all of us.

We tried to drive back winter, and winter won. Winter didn't just win; it dug in its heels and refused to leave. Wherever we looked, there was nothing but snow and ice. There was no way we could play soccer. Grounded or not, spring break was ruined. That's why when the final bell rang, none of us jumped for joy. All around us, kids were running to their freedom. But we walked very slowly, each one of us an island of despair and disappointment. The only sounds we heard were the sounds of our own footsteps plodding through the slush, and water dripping from the icicles on the roofs.

Although unplanned, we all gathered at the soccer field, sullen and defeated. We sat on the old bleachers and looked out over the snowy white soccer field and the trees bordering it, their branches heavy with snow. Larry's stand next to the entrance was still locked up tight, and the icicles on the gutters were dripping steadily into the puddles below.

In prior years, all this was different. In prior years, soccer season started the last day of school, the day Larry opened the stand. In prior years, this meant that for two whole weeks, we'd play soccer all day long. But all we could do this year was build a snowman. And Roger, oh my God, Roger the hero did just that. He built a snowman in April. I couldn't believe it. How could anyone know so little about life?

I looked at Tyler, who was sitting right next to me.

"This can't be it," he said softly. "This just can't be all there is."

He looked at Alex. Alex just got up, picked up his backpack, and left without a word. Danny followed him. He was grounded, too, and had to go home.

"Hey, Alex!" Roger yelled as he tried to put the second snowball onto the first to create his snowman's body. "I think this weather is brilliant."

And then Roger got what he deserved. He fell backwards onto his behind. The snowball exploded in his lap. All you could see in the heap of snow was Roger's head.

"Just imagine what it would be like if you were grounded for twenty days and the sun was shining. It could be a whole lot worse!" Roger tried to make us laugh, but Alex and Danny didn't even turn around.

"Come on," Diego said. "Let's get out of here."

But we stayed put and just stared at him. That's when Diego exploded with frustration. "This sucks!" he said, and walked away.

Everyone followed him. Everyone except me. I stayed put, tightly clutching the spare key to the hamster cage, shaking my head, totally worried things weren't going to get any better. And later, at home, when my dad was watching the news after dinner, I was still clutching that key.

The weather report finally came on. "Please," I thought, "please let it be spring." Next to me, Tyler kept his fingers crossed so tightly he almost tied them in a knot. But even

God wasn't listening. Better weather was not in the cards.

Later that night, I was in the top bunk. I clutched my new cleats in one hand, the key in the other. It was already past ten. Outside, drops from the icicles were splashing on the ground faster and faster, and I couldn't fall asleep.

"You know what, Tyler?" I asked.

"No," Tyler answered from the lower bunk. He was still awake, too.

"I really wanted to see it."

"See what?" Tyler asked.

"That bicycle kick. Oh man! You can't make this stuff up! A globe hits the living room wall, flies through the window, BAM! Right into his father's head! I wish I could have seen the look on his face."

"Whose face, Alex's?"

"Dude, I'm talking about his dad!" I had to laugh. I couldn't help it.

"What's so funny?" Tyler scolded me.

"Come on, no dumb questions. Picture his face," I said and leaned down over the edge, grinning down at Tyler.

For a few moments my brother was completely still. Then a grin spread across his face as his imagination took over. "Yeah. I can see it. BAM! at the living room wall. SMASH! through the window, and SMACK! right on the head." Tyler laughed, but then I was all serious again.

"*Now* what?" My brother asked, noticing.

"This can't be for nothing," I answered.

"Don't worry, it wasn't," Tyler responded. He grew all serious now, too. "Alex paid through the nose. He is grounded for twenty days."

"That's not what I mean," I said. "He sacrificed everything, you get it? Alex sacrificed himself. For us. He was *really* wild. A real... what's the word... a real martyrist, or something like that. And that can't be for nothing."

This time Tyler was quiet. Maybe he even agreed with me. Anyway, at some point I must have fallen asleep. I dreamed about Alex. I saw his bicycle kick. BAM! the globe hit the wall, SMASH! through the window, and SMACK! right into his father's head. I laughed and laughed and climbed into the sky alongside the globe, through the clouds, past the sun, and heading toward the stars. I circled around the moon twice before I crashed back down to earth, and the globe shattered.

"I don't like sad dreams," I was thinking while I was dreaming. But then something happened. The snow all around the globe melted away and the first daffodils poked through. It was amazing.

Tyler, the Pain!

The next morning something tickled my nose. I slowly opened my eyes and instantly shut them tight again. "Oh man, it hurts!" I blinked carefully at the blinding sunlight. The frost on our window had disappeared. What?! I leaped out of bed.

"Tyler!" I yelled, sliding down the ladder of our bunk bed. I pulled away his blanket. "Tyler! Wake up!" But Tyler was not there.

"Tyler?! Where are you?" I whirled around the room. "It's finally spring! Spring!"

I excitedly pointed toward the window. Tyler suddenly appeared in front of me, dressed in his soccer gear, grinning. Ready. "You don't say, sleepyhead," he said, and tossed my soccer gear at me. "Hurry up! Or else it'll be fall before we get to the soccer field."

I clocked a world record that day. That's how quickly I jumped out of my pj's and into my soccer gear. In a single stroke, all was right with the world again. Wow! I *had* been right. Alex's sacrifice had been worth it. When you're really wild, I realized, nothing bad will ever happen to you.

Unless you have a brother, and that brother is a pain. While I was working on my world record, Tyler took the spare key from my bed, unlocked the hamster cage, and grabbed my ball.

"See you at the soccer field, slowpoke!" he yelled, waved at me and ran out of the room with my ball.

"Hey, that's my ball!" I protested, and ran after him while I was still putting on my other shoe. "Stop!"

Tyler ignored me.

"You want it so bad, come and get it!" he yelled back, and ran down the stairs and into the dining room, where he almost collided with my dad, who was just coming out of the kitchen, coffee cup in hand.

"Watch out!" my dad grumbled, jumping out of the way at the last moment. Then he saw the soccer ball. "Whoa! Wait a minute! Stop right there! Where did this ball come from?"

"Oh! This ball? This is... Kevin's ball!" Tyler answered and ran through the kitchen out into the back yard. My dad turned towards the stairs. Bad idea. At precisely that moment, I jumped from the third step to the last step and right into him, and his coffee cup spilled and the hot liquid poured all over his shirt.

"Watch out!" he grumbled again.

"Yes, yes, I will!" I hissed impatiently. "But Tyler is right!"

"Really? Right about what?" Now my dad was really annoyed. "I know that ball. And it sure didn't fall from the sky."

"You're right, dad, it's my ball! You gave it to me for my birthday. Tyler, I'm warning you. Stop right now!" I yelled, slipping past my dad, running through the kitchen and out into the back yard, chasing down Tyler.

But Tyler was already in the street. Behind him, the garden gate banged shut. I flung it open and ran after him. That was *my* ball! The year's first shot on the soccer field was clearly mine, not my brother's. I ran as fast as I could, when suddenly someone shouted something to me: "Hey, slow down."

It was Tyler, calmly sitting on top of my ball, leaning against our back yard wall. I stopped dead in my tracks for a moment, then stomped over to him, steaming.

"That's my ball!" I hissed.

"No kidding," Tyler responded, grinning broadly.

"Then give it to me!" I was now standing directly in front of him.

"Not a chance!" Tyler grinned. "First, you have to thank me."

"Excuse me?" I could hardly believe my ears. "Are you nuts?!"

"No, but *you* are." Tyler kept on grinning. "What do you think Dad would have done if you just marched in there carrying your soccer ball? What would you say? 'Good morning, Dad, wow, it's perfect soccer weather today, so

thanks for forgetting all about the broken lamp and the
fact that we're grounded! We're going to go play now.' Do
you think he would have let you go?"

"Tight," I muttered under my breath so he couldn't
hear. Tyler was right for a change. The trick with the ball
was so clever. Wish I would have thought of it. But I
wasn't going to tell him that. "You're a pain, you know
that?" is what I said.

"Right back at you," Tyler said, got up and tossed the
ball to me. "Here! That's why we are brothers."

"Exactly!" I responded with a grin. "Unfortunately," and
threw the ball at his chest. Tyler caught it like a goalie.

I wouldn't expect anything less.

"Good shot!" he said. And then he took off.

"Hey! That's my ball," I yelled and ran after him.

"Then think fast!" Tyler laughed and tossed it back to me. That's how we ran all the way down the street. Happy.

Long Gone 'Cause Nothing Can Stop Us!

Of course spring didn't just hit Wilson Street this morning. All over town, against all odds, my friends' feet were itching to go, and every single one of them tried to get to the soccer field as early as they could.

Diego the tornado was not part of the great sacrifice we all made in our desperate fight against winter. He didn't break a lamp or shatter a window or destroy the world by bouncing it off his dad's forehead. He was in bed with the flu. That's why neither he nor Roger at 1236 Oak Park Avenue were grounded or banned from soccer. However, Diego was still not out of the woods as he stood in the kitchen of 11 St. Charles Street, squinting with total concentration at the thermometer in his mouth. Standing on the other side of the thermometer was his mother, doing the same.

"Below 99°!" she told Diego. "Below 99°, or no soccer!"

This was totally unfair and dumb. Yesterday he had to go to school with a 100° temperature. His mother claimed it was an entirely different story.

"Hmm. Different story, huh?" Diego thought, steaming with anger. He was so steamed he might have blown the top right off the thermometer. Luckily, he had thought of everything, including an ice cube under his tongue. Of course, his mother knew nothing about this cooling method. Saved by the beep! He grinned mischievously, and handed her the thermometer in a flash

"That's it then!" Diego said and ran out into the street.

"And stop worrying about me. I know exactly what I'm doing." His mother was stunned, but before she could protest he was long gone. She stared at the thermometer in disbelief. 91.5°! Not only did Diego no longer have a fever, he was now close to hypothermia!

Thanks to his ice cube trick Diego was the first to arrive at the soccer field, and the first to face the new, incredible, and practically insurmountable danger that was waiting for us.

Ten minutes earlier on Oak Park Avenue, Roger was about to bolt through the door.

"I'm going to the soccer field!" he yelled to his mother up in her office. "See you tonight!" But then, in an instant, all his enthusiasm and determination vanished from his face. Oh no! This can't be...!

"Hello, Roger darling! How sweet of you to wait for us!" Roger couldn't believe his eyes and ears. On the other side of the door were the three daughters of his mother's friends, forcing him back into the house like a wall of pink ribbons and lace.

"Mom! Are you kidding?" Roger yelled for help. "What are they doing here?"

But his mother was at the top of the stairs already, welcoming the girls, who barely had time to say "hello." They were already busy pinning a kicking-and-screaming Roger into a chair and torturing him with curlers.

"Mom! This is my last warning! Tell them to back off!" Roger threatened, but his mother ignored his pleas.

"Roger, what's all this fuss?" she said. She was visibly irritated, because she wanted to get back to work as quickly as possible. "Be glad that there's someone to play with. Your friends are all grounded."

"So what? You really think grounding them is going to stop them?" Roger responded. Now he had his back to the wall, but his mother just shrugged.

"I don't care what they do," she said. "You're staying here!"

With that, she vanished into her office. Roger turned and faced a wall of pink lace and ribbon. He was surrounded.

"But Roger darling, you are such a mess!" purred the three creatures from another planet in sugar sweet voices with acid tongues. He spoke very softly to them so his mother couldn't hear, every word cutting like a razor: "Listen carefully. Try to concentrate, because I'm not going to repeat myself. I am not your 'Roger darling.' And I am not a guinea pig for three pre-school stylists. Do I make myself clear?" With these words, Roger charged and blasted through the pink wall, and ran for his life and his freedom.

He ran and ran and arrived at the soccer field right after Diego, where he was next in line to face the humungous danger awaiting us.

Compared to Roger, Julian and Josh had an easy escape from Dearborn Street. They were a team, like Tyler and me. While their mother was in the bathroom getting ready for work, they begged and pleaded and whined at the door.

"Please Mom, the weather is so nice! You can't do this to us. The others are already on the soccer field. Their parents aren't this mean!"

Their mother remained steadfast, and when Julian and Josh wouldn't stop whining, she charged out of the bathroom to shut them up, only to find a boom box in the hallway blasting out her sons' whining voices. The real Julian and Josh were long gone. She caught a brief glimpse of them through the living room window as they ran down the street. They were making noise, but it didn't sound anything like whining.

Danny watched them run past his window from his living room in the house across the street. But unlike Julian and Josh, he wasn't smiling. He was concentrating as he stood dangerously perched on the back of a chair, which was dangerously perched on four unsteady towers of books. From there he hoped to snag his soccer ball from the top of the living room shelves without destroying his mother's expensive china.

Danny took a deep breath. He could just reach the

ball with the tips of his fingers. Carefully, very carefully, he lifted the ball. He had it! Suddenly the chair started tipping. Danny lost his balance. "Nooo!" he shouted, as two china plates slowly started rolling towards the edge of the top shelf. He let go of the ball and tried to regain his balance by performing a belly dance on the arm of the chair, and was about to jump off when the chair settled back down just as the plates fell and Danny caught them before they shattered on the marble floor.

Danny breathed a sigh of relief and wiped away the sweat with his arm. That's when his soccer ball teetered at the precipice, then rolled off the shelf and plummeted down, directly into the arms of his mother, who appeared out of nowhere, directly underneath him. Her stern look demanded an explanation.

"Phew!" he said, relieved. "That was close."

All he had left was an irresistible smile and with that smile, his best ideas. He stood there with that big old smile and offered her the plates. "Want to trade?" His mother just stared. Uncomfortable, he cleared his throat. Then he made one last ditch effort to save his own neck.

"Well, you know, I just thought, I..." he stammered.

"Get out!" His mother had finally lost her patience. "Right this instant!"

Danny grinned with relief.

"Oh man! I knew it. You are too cool. Did you know that, Mom?" With these words, he jumped off the chair,

placed the plates in his mother's hands, planted a kiss on her cheek, and stormed to the front door. That's when the phone rang. Danny automatically picked it up: "What's up? I'm in a hurry."

Silence on the other end of the line.

"Hello? Who is this?" Danny yelled, and when he recognized the breathing on the phone he became even more impatient.

"Alex, dude, knock it off!" Danny sighed. "I thought you'd be on the soccer field by now."

But Alex, who was at the other end of the line, watching his mother clean the house at fancy One Woodlawn Avenue, still didn't utter a word.

All Danny could hear was the vacuum.

"Oh man! You're grounded! I totally forgot. And you can't leave the house, am I right?"

Alex nodded but didn't say a word.

Danny rolled his eyes, waiting impatiently

"Alex, loser, I don't have time for this!"

But Alex remained silent, growing more and more desperate.

"Okay hold on," Danny said thinking fast. "Can you get to the bathroom?"

Silence. But Danny was on a roll.

"The bathroom window is directly above your garage. And next to the garage is that old apple tree. You know the one. Your dad wanted to chop it down but didn't have the heart? Are you listening? Do I have to draw you a map?"

Alex hung up. Message received. He dashed into the bathroom.

"About time!" Danny said and hung up.

Then he realized his mom had been watching him the whole time. Their eyes met. She was still holding the plates and the ball, looking at him with disapproval. He shrugged innocently.

"For gosh sakes, Mom, if he can't come up with it on his own, what am I supposed to do?" Then he flashed his best grin. "I guess I'll see you tonight, then!" He was the last to run out into the street and towards disaster.

Trapped!

All of us gathered one block away from the soccer field: Danny, Julian and Josh, Alex, Tyler, and me. We were laughing about being grounded and banned from soccer, and nobody was thinking about the consequences of our escape. That could wait until the evening. Until then, everything would be great. We felt fantastic as we stormed down the street. But when we took that last corner before the soccer field, we crashed into something that came towards us at full speed.

Danny hit the ground instantly. The rest of us pulled the brakes in time. All of us stared at the red-haired boy with the Coke-Bottle glasses and curlers in his hair.

"Oh my God, it's Roger!" Julian said.

"Of course it is," I said.

"Uh, Roger, you know the soccer field is the *other* way," laughed Josh, the youngest among us.

"That right?" Roger asked testily. He lost his temper and pushed Danny's hand away when he tried to help him up.

"What's up, man?" Danny asked, rubbing his own bump.

"Nada," Roger hissed. "We're too late. The soccer field is taken."

"No way!" Julian said.

"There you go again," I said to Roger, "Mr. Negativity."

"It's true." Roger stood in front of us, wringing his hands, eyes distorted by his Coke-bottle glasses, looking more like a cartoon character than a boy. "The soccer field *is* taken. *Really!* Today, for the next two weeks, probably forever."

Roger paused. He really seemed to expect us to keel over in shock. But we only looked at each other in disbelief. Roger got even angrier.

"Dang it, guys! Ask Diego if you don't believe me. He is stuck on the soccer field, too scared to move."

Now *that* was serious. Diego was not the kind of guy who'd joke around. Sometimes I even wondered if he would recognize a joke if it bit him on the butt. But that didn't matter now. Someone had taken our soccer field. And that was definitely no joke.

We immediately started running toward the field. Roger didn't budge. "No! Wait! Hold on! STOOOPP!" he yelled desperately. It sounded like we were running into a trap, but no one listened, we just kept on running. We ran down the street and right through the gate in the wooden fence that surrounds the soccer field. We ran past Larry's stand, where Larry was hopping off his scooter, getting ready to open up for the season. And we ran towards Diego, who sat smack in the middle of the field at the center mark, wheezing in fear.

Diego didn't say a word. He was desperately fighting back his asthma. Probably a grass allergy, I thought, because there was nothing else around that could have done this to him. The soccer field was empty. It was completely empty, except for us and Roger, who had finally appeared at the gate, flailing his arms wildly.

"Guys! Come back while you still have a chance!" he shouted.

We looked at each other. We didn't get it. It just didn't make any sense. I was just about ready for the next round of insults when *something* moved all around us.

At first I thought, cockroaches. Giant cockroaches. But even Asian cockroaches aren't that big. No, they were boys. Just like us. Only bigger. And stronger. And fatter. And they came running at us. Roger was just ahead of them and hid among us, scared to death. And he had every right to be. These guys surrounding us were grim, scary, fearless and cool. Viciously cool. We caught our breath and our hearts skipped a beat when, just as Roger had warned, Mickey the bulldozer appeared.

Never Give Up!

Mickey the bulldozer was the Darth Vader of our world. And when Mickey appeared at the gate of our soccer field, that's who was glaring at us from the t-shirt that barely covered Mickey's fat belly. Yet unlike Darth Vader, the bulldozer did not wear a science-fiction mask.

Mickey's face was real. If you could call it a face. His tiny beady eyes sat like black coals between beefy cheeks, and his breath rattled like an elephant seal just coming up for air.

Mickey the bulldozer was the coolest and the toughest guy at our school and in our neighborhood, and he was afraid of nothing and nobody. There was a simple reason for this. Mickey didn't travel alone. Like the way garbage attracts flies, Mickey attracts other jerks, and they approached us now from all sides.

The bulldozer waited at the gate like the commander of his troops, never moving an inch. Oozing confidence, he waited until his soldiers had moved into position.

They surrounded us, leering at us. Humungous Henry, who was even fatter than Mickey. Hard to imagine, right? Octopus, the tallest of them all, had arms that reached almost all the way to the ground. I saw Juggernaut Jim, Mow-down, and Rick the grim reaper, who wore a bicycle chain around his neck and on his bare chest like a bandolier. And then there was Kong, the monumental creature from the prairies of Mongolia.

I heard that guy was strong enough to rip high voltage lines apart with his bare hands. But none of those jerks were as strong or as mean as Mickey. And he was coming right at us.

He stomped across the wet field; his every step turned the muddy water to steam. The ground shook. So did his flabby paunch. But underneath all that fat were iron muscles and a black heart. We automatically backed up and wanted to run, but Grim Reaper and Kong formed a brick wall behind us.

Mickey the bulldozer stood over Diego, still sitting at the center mark, agitated and wheezing. Mickey pushed him into the mud and kept on coming. All the rumors we'd ever heard about him were unwinding in my head. I could almost see that bulldog, dripping fangs and all, as it leaped at Mickey. That's exactly how they say it happened three years ago. That bulldog should have been registered as a lethal weapon and when it charged Mickey at full speed, it would have ripped a normal human being limb from limb. But Mickey grabbed it by its ears and hurled it over his shoulder through the air, and when it crashed into the earth it kept running and never looked back. And Mickey just stood there smiling, holding a bulldog ear in each hand. That was when Mickey was ten and barely out of third grade. Now he was thirteen and two heads taller than any of us.

I looked around me to see if there was anyone who could help us. In the movies this would be a perfect time for a superhero to show up and save the day. But other than us, the only person on the soccer field was Larry, and he was busy taking the barricades off his stand, quietly and calmly, as if nothing out of the ordinary was going on at all.

I actually liked Larry. He was the best adult in the whole wide world. He never treated us like kids and he never talked down to us. In his eyes we were real men already, who could decide their own destiny. Apparently that's what he thought at the moment as well, and today I cursed him for that.

Frankly, I didn't *want* to decide my own destiny just then. I wanted to be who I really was: a nine-year-old boy. Or invisible. That's what you want when Mickey the bulldozer is stomping towards you, shaking the earth, towering in front of you like a skyscraper. I stared into the mask of Darth Vader on his fat belly then moved my gaze up slowly and looked into his glowing eyes.

"Damn, we're trapped by this moron!" Danny cursed next to me. I didn't tell him this, but I felt a whole lot better knowing he was next to me. But Humungous Henry didn't like it at all.

"Did you hear that?" he screeched. "Mickey, did you hear what he called you?"

"Shut up!" the Bulldozer commanded and snapped his fingers. "Octopus!"

Octopus launched the ball in a heartbeat and the Bulldozer caught it and thundered it against Danny's chest, pounding him into the ground gasping for air.

"I have ears, Humungous!" the Bulldozer grinned and easily caught the ball that bounced back from Danny's chest. "Octopus didn't hear it good, want to repeat that?" he said to Danny.

Danny just glared at him angrily, but kept quiet, and none of us could blame him for that. Then the Bulldozer took a step towards me.

"Good! Then we understand each other. As of today, this soccer field belongs to us and only we get to play here. We're the *Unbeatables*."

All the morons roared and Mickey just stood there looking triumphant.

"*Unbeatables*, did you hear that?" he threatened. "And as of this nanosecond, all you measly midgets can get lost. You got no business here anymore."

The Bulldozer looked at us as if he could vaporize us with a look. Even if we wanted it, that wasn't going to happen. We couldn't leave. This was our soccer field and we weren't going to give it up, no matter how many tough-talking morons showed up.

"What's wrong? Didn't you understand me?" Mickey the bulldozer mocked us. "Should I ask Kong to make things crystal clear for you?"

Kong stepped forward enthusiastically and signaled his willingness by cracking his knuckles with an inhuman bone-cracking noise.

"No," I said quickly, "that's not necessary," and the Bulldozer grinned with satisfaction.

"What do you know! The midget knows how to talk!" Mickey laughed spitefully and the other morons chimed in.

"Then I don't get why you're not telling your fellow midgets to beat it? What are you waiting for?" he hissed and threw my soccer ball against my chest.

I stumbled but didn't fall to the ground. The Bulldozer caught the ball again.

"Not a chance," I countered defiantly.

The grin on Mickey's face vanished.

"What did you say? I didn't quite get that!" he hissed and threw the ball at my chest a second time and this time I fell to the ground. Mickey caught it.

"I said, 'not a chance,'" I hissed. "You heard me."

"Excuse me?!" Mickey's face was bright red. He reached back to throw the ball a third time. "I don't think you know what you are saying!" he screamed and thundered it at me.

But this time I caught it like a goalie, jumped up instantly and shot it back at that fat tub of goo.

"I know exactly what I'm doing!" I screamed back. "I'm going to give you two weeks, you towering tub of goo! Two weeks and not a day more. That's how long you and your morons have to pretend that this soccer field is yours. Then we'll be back for a challenge. And we won't just be cracking our knuckles. We'll be playing soccer. You think you're unbeatable? Then prove it in two weeks. If you win, then the field is yours, as long as a soccer ball is round. But if we win, then you take your morons and go play someplace else. If we win, this soccer field is ours, once and for all, forever. Is that clear?"

I shoved the soccer ball into Mickey's flabby belly and it made him burp. My friends looked at me in disbelief.

Maybe they were already writing my obituary. They had to think I was suicidal or crazy, or both. Only Danny whistled through his teeth.

"Dude! That was... *wild!*"

We were surrounded by giants: Humungous, the Grim Reaper, Octopus, and Kong, and they were waiting for the command from the Bulldozer to take us out. Their eyes locked on him and so did ours.

The Bulldozer was stunned. The color in his face changed like a traffic light. Then he burped again, and this burp morphed into a strange uncomfortable laugh that grew louder and louder.

"Did you hear that?" he laughed. "Did you all hear that? The midget barely reaches to my belly button, but he spits in my face."

Then he became really serious and looked at me as if he wanted to kill me. For the first time I started doubting my own sanity in saying what I had said. But I made sure it didn't show. Instead I met his gaze and asked: "What's up? Are you afraid?"

Mickey's eyes narrowed, if that's even possible. All I heard was his rasping breath. Then he answered: "I don't even know what fear is."

He said it in a way that at that moment I knew exactly what fear is. I tried to swallow it, but it wasn't working. I could feel my knees buckle. Luckily, the Bulldozer began to laugh: "OK! Deal! We'll see you in two weeks. Right here!"

I looked from the Bulldozer to Danny and Tyler in disbelief. They couldn't believe it either. Then we didn't risk staying another second. We turned on our heels and ran. We ran past Larry's stand through the gate, and we shouted and cheered as if we had already won the game.

With Bated Breath

The minute we were outside the soccer field we broke down laughing.

"*Unbeatables?* More like bunch of losers!" Roger laughed.

"I'll give you two weeks, you towering tub of goo!" Danny copied me, and Diego, whose asthma had miraculously disappeared, finished the sentence with enthusiasm: "That's how long you and your morons get to pretend you own our soccer field!"

"Dude! That was wild!" Julian laughed, shaking his head.

"Yeah, totally wild!" Josh laughed, and Roger got right to the heart of what we were all thinking: "They're shaking in their boots! These losers won't know what hit them!"

But Alex and my brother Tyler weren't saying anything. They were staring through the wooden fence, watching the *Unbeatables* start their training.

The Bulldozer ran up to the ball and then thundered it towards the goal. Inside the net, Octopus was flying, reaching for the ball with his tentacles; he had no trouble catching it at all.

"Hey Octopus!" Roger shouted, "What kind of lame ball was that? Even I could have caught it."

Octopus and the Bulldozer looked over at us and didn't say a word. Octopus just casually tossed the ball to the Bulldozer, and he kicked it. But this time he didn't aim at the goal. He aimed at us. The ball hit the wooden fence so hard that one of the planks splintered into a thousand pieces.

Alex the cannon, the man with the world's strongest kick, swallowed hard with respect. The rest of us remained perfectly still. Only Roger said: "Losers!"

But just like the rest of us, he watched them with bated breath. How were we supposed to win against these guys? Winter still sat in our bones. We hadn't played together in months, and now we didn't even have the field to practice on. Mickey the bulldozer and his *Unbeatables*, on the other hand, could practice every day. And it wasn't just that they were four or five years older than us. There was more.

Every single one of them had a reputation that made your blood run cold. And obviously their stupidity didn't keep them from playing soccer.

Our laughter had caught in our throats. Diego had started coughing again, and with heads hanging low, we slumped down on the curb. We continued our silence until I couldn't stand it anymore. But my brother Tyler beat me to it.

"This isn't going to work!" he said. "We need a plan."

"Okay, what did you have in mind?" Julian asked.

"Use some of your magic to make a new soccer field for us out of thin air?"

Tyler just shrugged his shoulders. "There will always be a place to play. I'm talking about something else."

"What?"

"A coach," Tyler said calmly. "If we want to beat these jerks — and we don't really have a choice after the performance you put on today — if we want to beat these jerks, someone has to coach us."

Every single one of us looked at him, stunned. That's Tyler. If he built a house, he'd start with the roof.

"Don't you think we have a few more important problems right now?" I asked him, irritated. He just gave me the once over.

"If you ask me, we only have one problem: we are scared stiff. We all look like we just wet our pants."

"Smart Aleck!" I teased. "Don't make me laugh."

Danny came to my aide: "You know, your brother Tyler is a real pain."

Silence. Deep down inside we both knew that Tyler was right. We just didn't want to admit it.

"Fine!" Tyler mocked us. "Then let's just sit here until our two weeks are up. Then what? I'll tell you what. You'll all go into hiding!"

"Very funny," Roger yelled, but one glance from Tyler and he shut up.

"Maybe. But even if we were allowed to play in Toyota Park, we'd be hiding under our beds."

No one said a word. Tyler was right. Toyota Park wouldn't help us win. A different soccer field wouldn't make the *Unbeatables* lose. The Bulldozer's kick would not be softer, Octopus would not be less fearsome, the Grim Reaper wouldn't be nicer and Kong and Mow-down would not slow down. Tyler was on to something. We needed to improve our own play. In fact, a coach was a brilliant idea. But like any brilliant idea, execution was key.

Who could train us? Who would want to train us? Roger mentioned the U.S. Soccer coach Bob Bradley. I think he was the only coach Roger knew by name. We didn't even bother discussing him.

The only man we knew of who had ever played soccer was Alex's dad. But Alex was afraid to go home. He was grounded for twenty days and the last thing he wanted to do was ask his father a question.

Then someone we knew limped towards us. "Hello men!" he greeted us. "I may be wrong but I'm betting today was a really tough day for you!"

Then he winked knowingly and handed each of us a lemonade.

"If there's anything I can do, just say the word!" he smiled. We liked his smile, you can bet your life on it, no matter how much he reeked of beer.

Larry, of Course!

Suddenly it was as clear as day.

"Larry, of course!" we shouted and jumped up.

Larry stepped back in shock. He had not seen that much excitement in years.

"You used to be a soccer pro, right?" Danny shouted.

"Now wait a minute, hold your horses!" Larry tried to slow us down.

"Yes, you said so yourself!" I interrupted.

"You sure did!" agreed Josh.

"Of course he was!" confirmed Roger. "He was the best! Just look at him!"

Larry stood before us and tried to wipe his eight-day-stubble from his wrinkled face. He was clearly embarrassed.

"Hold on, you're moving too fast, wait just one darn minute!" he stammered.

We hung at his lips. Larry took off his baseball cap and wiped the sweat off his brow.

"Well, to be honest, I..."

"No, you said so!" Diego cut him off. He didn't want to hear the rest of the sentence. "You used to be a real pro, until a browbeater like Mickey the bulldozer ruined your knee."

Larry stood in front of us and helplessly shrugged his shoulders.

"Did I really say that?"

We nodded and looked at him, silently. Larry cleared his throat.

"I might have had a few when I said that."

We shook our heads.

"Honestly? Are you sure?"

We smiled at him in anticipation. Larry sighed. Then he did a dance that looked as if he wanted to jump out of his skin. Finally, he was done with it.

"OK, fine," he sighed, "you're looking for a coach. Did I get that right?"

"Yup, you did," Tyler answered expectantly.

"And you chose me?" Larry was skeptical.

"Yup, we did," Danny and I blurted out.

"Why?" Larry asked. "Because you don't have anyone else?"

We didn't respond. We were embarrassed.

"Or because you really believe that I'm the best man for the job?"

We just looked at him.

"You have to be honest with me now. What you just did, Kevin, was crazy. You're lucky you didn't get a black eye."

"No big deal," I grinned, but Larry locked eyes with me and wiped that grin right off my face.

"You know the only thing the bunch of you is going to get in two weeks is a black eye. You'll be lucky if that's *all* you get. Mickey the bulldozer and his *Unbeatables* are way out of your league."

We looked up at him, surprised. That's not what we expected, or rather, that's not what we wanted to hear. But Larry showed no mercy.

"And if you ask me, you don't stand a chance against them."

That was too much for me. I jumped up.

"You bite! I thought you were our coach!" I exploded, but Larry just shook his head.

"Not yet I'm not. Right now, I'm just a friend who is being honest with you."

"We can live without your honesty, thank you very much! In fact, why don't you just kiss my butt!" I was hopping mad and I had to fight back the tears.

Larry looked from me to the others, who were still sitting in front of him at the curb.

"Do you agree with Kevin?" he asked. The others looked at the ground, embarrassed.

"OK," Larry said, "then maybe I can't help you."

He picked up the empty glasses and limped back to the soccer field. We looked after him. We were shattered. Then Larry stopped and turned around.

"I thought you wanted to beat those jerks," Larry challenged us.

I had no clue what was going on.

"What do you mean?" I shouted, "I thought you said it was impossible."

"Probably," Larry answered calmly. "But even the impossible is possible if you are honest." A gentle smile played around his lips, but that made me even more furious.

"OK, OK, and what is it exactly you want to hear?" What I was about to say I had never said in my whole nine years: "Yes, I'm scared. I'm scared stiff! Is that it? Are you happy now?"

Larry's smile vanished. He shook his head sadly. "No, I'm not. I want to know what kind of coach you want. If you want *me*, then you have to trust me one hundred percent. And I have to trust you one hundred percent. Trusting each other is the only way we can beat the *Unbeatables*."

Larry just stood there, waiting.

Diego swallowed hard: "And what about our fear?" That question had been on all our minds.

"I understand," Larry nodded, and his smile put dimples on his cheeks. "Your fear is fantastic. It is because of your fear that you even have a chance. Don't you get that? Your fear is your strength."

We shook our heads. We didn't get a word he was saying.

Larry took off his cap and scratched his head.

"Dang! Aw, who cares, you'll get it eventually. The main thing is that tomorrow you'll all come to the park near the lake. There's a field right at the dock. At ten. Is that clear? Whoever is late pays for a round of beer... oops, I mean lemonade. And keep your chin up, men!"

Larry winked at us one more time, and then started limping toward his stand. It took another quick minute for us to realize we actually had a coach. That took a huge load off my mind.

"We'll be there!" I yelled after Larry. "You can rely on us one hundred percent!"

"And you *Unbeatables*," Roger yelled through the fence to the soccer field. "Watch out! Mickey, tell your morons! You have two weeks, and not a second more."

And then we ran.

Moms and Dads

We ran like mad. This was a fantastic day. We had shown
Mickey the bulldozer who was boss, and we had our very
own coach. We were no longer just a few little boys, but
a full-blown soccer team with a decisive match ahead.
We wanted to tell everybody about it. We *had* to tell
everybody, and so we ran home as quickly as we could.
Including Alex. And that was a mistake.

Alex had forgotten what had happened the past few
days. But it all came back to him when he stood in front
of One Woodlawn Avenue.

"Grounded for twenty days," the echo in his head was
painful, "and a total ban on soccer!" Clever as he was, he
decided against the front door and opted for the route
that included the apple tree and the garage. After all, it
wasn't even lunch time, maybe his mother hadn't even
noticed he was gone yet. But when he crawled through
the window into the bathroom, there was his father sitting
on the toilet. Just like clockwork, Alex's father had come
home for lunch, and when he saw his son come in through
the bathroom window, his sense of humor went out.

"Get to your room!" he ordered flatly. "We will talk later."

Talk? What was there to talk about? All Alex did was play soccer. Tomorrow morning at ten, practice was supposed to begin. *Had* to begin.

Danny had the least problems. His mother sent him away herself to save her china. She had no good reason to be angry. And as he was excitedly telling her the whole story now, she just shook her head. "Why does a man always have to do what a man has to do?" she wondered. "Your father will like that, you'll have to tell him about it tonight." That was it for Danny. All he had to do was wait for morning to come and practice to start. But then his mother asked one more question. "What will you do if Alex doesn't show up?"

At the same time, Diego stormed into the kitchen of 11 St. Charles Street, where his mother was waiting for him. She stood there, holding the thermometer in her hand. At first, Diego thought he had traveled through time and was back where he started when he played the ice cube under the tongue trick on her this morning. Just to be sure, he checked the clock. No, it was really noon, thereby proving with absolute certainty, his mother had not moved in three hours.

"Oh man, Mom, don't you have anything better to do?" The words just slipped out of Diego's mouth instead of a "hello." But his mother didn't say a word. That's why he knew something else with absolute certainty: she hadn't quite bought his earlier temperature ruse. She wanted to take his temperature one more time, and this time Diego did not have an ice cube under his tongue.

The situation was hopeless. He took the thermometer and put it in his mouth. 99° was the magic number. The numbers on the thermometer climbed higher and higher. When they reached 98.5° he closed his eyes, but an eternity passed until the beep finally went off.

"100°!" his mother said. It sounded like a death sentence.

"I want Dr. Gilberto Muñoz from the Chicago Fire!" he protested. "This is a no-brainer for him. He'll treat me and I'll be fine in no time!"

"Off to bed!" was his mother's clear and definite answer.

"Mom, I don't think you get the most important things in life!" Diego responded. And although he was sure he was right, his protest fell on deaf ears and he went to bed like a good little boy.

Roger, on the other hand, was not at all a good little boy. He had no intention of being a good little boy. Roger was mad. When he returned to 1236 Oak Park Avenue, his mother's friend's three daughters were still standing in front of the chair, fussing over their own hair.

"If any of you calls me Roger darling, you're getting a wedgie!" With that impressive threat he stormed past, up the stairs and into his mother's office. "Now I need you to listen carefully! Mickey the bulldozer has us by the throat and they took over the soccer field for the next two weeks. That's why we have to trust each other and win, no matter what the cost. And that's why I can't be bothered with these silly cows down there, do you read me?"

His mother stopped typing, flabbergasted, but said nothing.

"OK, so we agree!" Roger answered for her, and stormed out of the room. "Hey you, I mean the three pre-school stylists down there," he shouted down at the girls from the top of the stairs. "Your granny's poodle ripped your Barbie dolls to shreds!"

Horrified, the girls jumped up and rushed to the front door.

"And I helped! It was fun! Don't let the door hit you on the way out."

The girls stormed out, screaming. Then it was quiet. Roger listened at his mother's office door. She was back to her typing. He grinned with satisfaction and ceremoniously took the last curler out of his hair.

Half an hour later, Julian and Josh's mother came home from work and went to the kitchen to have a talk with her sons. But what she found there on the kitchen table on Dearborn was not her sons, but the boom box. Julian and Josh's mother sighed, and turned it on.

"We are waiting for you in the tree house." Their announcement was short and precise.

Julian and Josh's mother hesitated for a moment. She bit her lip and deeply furrowed her brow. Then she boldly walked to the kitchen door, flung it open, and yelled towards the tree house. "No way!"

But the tree house remained still and quiet. Julian and Josh's mother was determined now: "Julian and Josh! I know you are hiding up there. I expect you back in the kitchen on the count of three!"

She marched back into the kitchen with resolve and started counting slowly. Her voice was loud and clear:

"One!"

"Two!"

"Two and a half..."

"Three!"

But the tree house remained still and quiet. Instead, the boom box started again.

"Dear mom, even if you count to one hundred, we will not come to the kitchen."

Julian and Josh's mother whirled around, and with a "Just you wait, you're going to be sorry you messed with me!" she stormed out into the yard and climbed up the tree house. It wasn't all that easy. The tree house was not only built by kids, but for kids. It had three levels. Julian and Josh's mother forced herself up through every floor, climbed stairs that were too small for grown-up feet, tiptoed over wooden planks that were too narrow, mounted terrace after terrace. She was knocked, scratched, and pinched at every level, and she kept repeating: "Just you wait, you're going to be sorry you messed with me!"

With these words she finally forced open the door to the top floor of the tree house and froze. In front of her was a table set for dinner, and her two sons were waiting next to it. Josh, wearing her apron, balanced a pizza on his hand, and Julian, who wore a tie over his t-shirt, held a bottle of red wine. Julian and Josh's mother got out her "Just you wait!" then swallowed the rest of her words, as her two sons beamed at her.

"Mom, you are right, we do need to talk about something," Julian smiled and Josh blurted out: "But it's not what you think."

Their mother looked from one to the other.

"Really... and what am I not thinking?"

"What Kevin did," Josh's words just flew out of his mouth. "He showed Mickey the bulldozer who's boss, and we're all going to get a black eye because of it. Maybe even more. That's why we have to practice hard every day. With Larry, he'll show us all the tricks we need to learn to beat them."

Their mother sat down, more confused than before.

"Just a moment. Who is Mickey the bulldozer?" she wanted to know.

"He's the guy who tears off dogs' ears!" Josh responded as Julian poured her a glass of wine.

"Have a drink and eat something first," he smiled. "And then we'll talk about being banned from soccer. You don't want us to lose the soccer field to Darth Vader, do you?"

I asked my dad a very similar question. We were sitting at the dinner table on Wilson Street. He took my ball back as soon as he got home from work. The last soccer ball the *Wild Bunch* had left! He took it straight to his office. And that's where it was now, locked up securely. It was three minutes to the news, and my dad still didn't say a word.

"You know, dad, you really have to give the ball back," I said in the most matter-of-fact voice I could muster. "The cleaning lady is still sick and there is nobody else who can unlock the door for us."

My dad choked on his beer and sprayed it all over his shirt. "Excuse me? Would you repeat that?" he snorted.

"I just want us to be completely honest with each other, you know? Only if we are honest and sincere can we defeat Mickey the bulldozer, and for that we need the ball."

I smiled at my dad. My dad looked at me, and then at my brother.

"Honest and sincere?" he asked and Tyler smiled back.

"All right," my dad said. "You can have your ball, but only under one condition."

Tyler and I nodded enthusiastically.

"You have to take Sox with you to practice," he said, his voice just as matter-of-fact as mine was earlier.

"Oh no, that won't work! We have to practice! Sox will ruin everything!" we both protested, but my dad remained firm.

"Honest and sincere, you said," he smiled. "You said it yourself. Sox is your dog. And way back when I bought him, that's the promise you gave me. 'We will take good care of him every day,' you said."

Dad was right. We were quiet and looked at Sox, embarrassed. He was lying in his basket, looking back at us, wagging his tail. "How are we going to make this work?" Tyler and I wondered. Sox would run after every ball like it was a mailman. That's what dogs do.

Diego was in bed with a fever, and Alex...? My God, what about Alex? How could we possibly beat the *Unbeatables* without him?

"Dad, we have to go out again," we yelled, and hurried out into the street. We picked up Danny, Josh, Julian, and Roger, and the six of us ran over to One Woodlawn Avenue.

Alex was in his room, sitting on his bed. His father stood in front of him, talking. He talked and talked. How disappointed he was in his son, how little he respected his own father, and how downright rude he was. In the end he demanded an explanation for it all. But Alex didn't talk. That's why his father started talking yet again. He talked and talked, and then he explained that it was necessary to resort to more drastic measures.

"That's why, my dear son, you will spend all of your spring break here in your room. Is that clear?"

Alex's father stood in front of his son and waited for an answer. But as usual, Alex didn't say a word. He just sat on his bed and looked right through his father out the window. That's when we rang the doorbell. And we kept ringing.

"What do you want?" Alex's father asked when he opened the door.

"We want to save the day. We're the superheroes!" Josh grinned.

"And we can explain everything!" Tyler added.

"It's about honor and pride!" I said.

"And we have to be honest and sincere!" Julian hurried to say, while kicking Danny in the shin.

"Yes, ahh, right," Danny stuttered. "I was the one who told Alex how to escape. You know, the garage and the apple tree — you know the one you always wanted to get rid of? That's why you can't blame Alex."

"Yes, and that's why Danny will share his punishment," Roger chimed in.

Danny riveted him with a chilling look. Being grounded voluntarily was just too much, and for the first time I noticed that Roger didn't have a free pass with Danny after all. Roger felt it too, and it made him nervous.

"No, seriously, Mr. Cannon, and ahh, I mean we'll all help him, of course. You know, that means we all want to be grounded just like Alex. All of us!"

Alex's father raised his brow. He had never heard of such a thing. And to be honest with you, neither had we. We all looked at Roger as if he had just escaped from the funny farm, and that made him even more nervous.

"Yes, seriously, that's precisely what we want, Mr. Cannon, but only if we can postpone the whole thing for a very short while. We would be available to serve our sentence in say, two weeks? What do you think?"

Roger managed a smile, realizing he had almost messed the whole thing up. We thought so, too.

"Without Alex, we'll never win!" he blurted one last time.

Alex's father just stared at us. Seconds passed, minutes, and hours. At least it felt like it. We were about to take a hike when Alex's father cleared his throat and finally said: "OK, fine."

Alex's father, who usually talks up a storm, said nothing more that day.

The First Touch

In soccer, sometimes the first touch of the ball can decide everything. That was particularly true for Diego the next day. Really early in the morning, about seven, he tiptoed into the kitchen of 11 St. Charles Street, took three ice cubes from the freezer, and put them in his mouth. He was sure it would be enough until his mother got up — and then nothing would stand in the way of practice.

He closed the freezer door and danced out of the kitchen. But his mother stood in the doorway, and her expression told Diego that he was trapped. He fearfully swallowed all three ice cubes at once and stammered, "Hello Mom, um, I mean good morning!" His breath formed frost on the pot that was sitting on the stove six feet away.

Luckily his mother didn't notice. She approached him and looked into his open mouth as he continued to hold his icy breath. Then she put the thermometer between his teeth.

"Did you really think I'd fall for your little scam twice in a row?" she asked and left the kitchen.

Diego pulled the thermometer from his mouth, and

took as deep a breath as he could. Then he put the thermometer back into his mouth.

"Don't breathe, no matter what! Don't breathe, no matter what!" he told himself over and over. "If you breathe now, the thermometer will freeze to your lips."

Seconds passed. First ten. Then twenty, then thirty, and finally forty. Diego stopped counting. His eyes bulged from the lack of oxygen and finally his mother came back into the kitchen. Diego was sure he'd explode at any moment. The thermometer would fly out of his mouth and — just like Iceman's ice cannon — his breath would freeze his mother and the entire apartment.

That's when he was finally saved by the beep. In a flash he pulled the thermometer from his mouth, handed it to his mother, turned around and blew out his arctic air and took another deep breath. When his breath hit a fly, it fell to the ground, killed by frost.

"Oh God!" Diego said.

"You can say that again!" his mother confirmed. "Only God knows how you do that!"

"Do what?" Diego asked innocently as he turned towards her. "How high?"

"98.2!" his mother answered as skeptically as if the thermometer had said the sky was purple.

But Diego was already rushing to his room.

Just like us. Tyler and I were in a terrible hurry. My dad was out taking Sox for a walk, and it would just be bad timing if we were gone when he came back. As much as we loved and cared for Sox, we simply didn't want him around during practice.

At 9:00 AM sharp we were all at the park by the lake. Of course we knew that practice didn't start until an hour later, but we couldn't wait any longer. So we just started to kick the ball around. I kicked it high up in the sky. Then we ran. Every one of us wanted to get to the ball first, but I tell you, none of us did.

Right at the start, Diego slipped and fell face first into the muck. Josh and Roger couldn't even move. They were stuck in the mud up to their ankles, as if they had glue on their feet. Julian and Tyler started to run, but they didn't get far. They stumbled over the stones that were all over the grass. And finally, Diego, Alex and I plunged into a knee-deep hole filled to the brim with water.

"Bravo! Bravo!" somebody clapped. I crawled out of the hole and saw Larry sitting on a tree trunk just a few feet away from us.

"This is no soccer field!" I yelled at him and Julian rubbed his knee. "We'll break our necks here!"

"That's for sure!" Roger moaned desperately. He was still stuck. "Just look at us."

"I am looking at you," Larry grinned, amused, but I didn't think this was funny at all.

"Wipe that grin off your face!" I spat at him. "You can't practice here! The only thing you can do here is...!" I was so mad that I couldn't think of anything to say. "The only thing you can do here is...!"

"Learn to swim?" Larry filled in the blanks.

I sucked in a lungful of air. I was ready to put a curse on him, but Larry beat me to it.

"I think the water is still too cold for swimming. That's why I suggest you first learn how to run."

He limped towards my ball and kicked it to the other end of the field.

"We won't need that yet."

We stared at him in utter disbelief. How could we practice without a soccer ball? But Larry ignored our protests. "You don't think that Mickey the bulldozer and his *Unbeatables* will play fair, do you? That's why for right now, you're going to run a race. Always in pairs. And while you are running, imagine that the stones and holes are the legs of those jerks. They will foul you; you know that, don't you? That's why you'll dodge them, jump right over them, and dance between them."

"You got to be kidding!" Danny yelled and wiped the mud off his face. "The mud is as slippery as an ice rink."

"Exactly!" Larry said. "I almost forgot about the mud. The mud is your fear. The fear and the wobbly knees you'll have when someone like Mow-down, Juggernaut, or Kong is running towards you."

"They don't scare me," snapped Julian. "I'll just take the ball from him." His eyes glittered with fury. When soccer was at stake, Julian feared no one. Larry let out a sigh.

"Look," he said and picked up a small pebble. "This pebble, that's you, and the big boulder over there, that's the *Unbeatables*."

Then he threw the pebble as hard as he could. The small pebble bounced off the boulder and came flying back. Larry looked at Julian.

"You will learn what fear is," he said.

Julian looked to the ground, embarrassed, but Larry didn't stand for it.

"Unless, you learn to use the pebble's advantage," he said. "The pebble is quick and nimble and light as a feather. The pebble can dance."

Larry tossed a second pebble. This time he tossed it flatly. The stone landed in a puddle, bounced up and over the big boulder, bounced up again and over three more big chunks of stone.

We finally got it. A smile played on our lips, and we ran off. No matter how often we slipped, fell, plunked into puddles or scraped our knees and elbows, nobody gave up. We raced each other over and over again. In the end we even did it blindfolded. And when Larry turned on his boom box, nobody protested. With blindfolded eyes we moved to the rhythm of the music. To us, the muddy field seemed smoother than a golf course, and we danced all over it like laughing elves.

In the end, Larry sprang for lemonade, which he had brought from his stand, and although we were all exhausted, we couldn't stop laughing. In our minds, we pictured how the Bulldozer or Humungous or scary Kong stood in front of Larry's stand, locked up because Larry was here with us. We imagined how they'd fall to their knees, sweat pouring down their faces, how they'd hammer against the stand, begging, eyes to the heavens, pleading for something to drink.

Oh man, life was beautiful, especially when Larry told us we'd finally get to play with a ball the next day. We all felt fabulous and after that first day, nobody had any doubt that we'd beat Mickey the bulldozer and his *Unbeatables*.

A Moment of Truth

But the next morning, everything was different. I wanted to jump out of bed, but the pain in my legs forced me back. At first I thought something was seriously wrong, but then I realized that I was just really sore. I struggled down the bunk bed ladder. Tyler was no better. We had to tie each other's shoes. We just couldn't reach our own feet. We limped out of the house. Just like the day before, we wanted to leave before our dad came home from his walk with Sox. But he was still home, waiting in the backyard, holding out Sox's leash.

"No, please don't," we moaned.

Our dad surprisingly just shrugged his shoulders.

"OK," he said, and we sighed a breath of relief, "but then I get the ball. That was the deal."

"No, no way!" I yelled. "We need it today. Absolutely. Larry said so."

"Good. And Sox needs you!" my dad said, Sox sitting right beside him, wagging his tail, as if he wanted to sweeten our harsh fate.

We were furious, because we knew what that wagging tail meant: attack the ball. We knew we wouldn't be able to play a normal game because every time the ball goes into play, Sox bites deeper into it. It was only a matter of time until our last soccer ball would be ruined, too. And so, before that could happen, I grabbed Sox and tied him to the best tree I could find. Sox yelped and howled, but I didn't care. My sore muscles had made me angry, and all I wanted to do now was play soccer. But just as soon as I had tied up Sox, Larry arrived for practice, and took the ball away from me. He kicked it high in the air, all the way to the other end of the field and said, just like yesterday:

"We won't need it today."

I completely lost it.

"Excuse me?" I yelled. "But yesterday you said we would. You said that we'd play with a ball today. Didn't he?"

The others nodded. So I was right and Larry was a liar. I stubbornly stormed off to get my ball, but Larry stopped me in my tracks.

"Wait, Kevin," he said. "I didn't say you couldn't play with a ball today. Here you go."

Larry grinned, and showed us what he was holding. We were horrified.

"That's not a ball," I said.

"Sure, it is," Larry said, "I believe around these parts we call it a tennis ball."

"You can't play soccer with a tennis ball," I countered.

"Yes, you can, if that's all you have. Way back when, we used to play with tin cans and stones."

"Big deal!" I complained. "We have something better. Over there, that's my ball. I had to bring Sox with me because of that ball, and because of that ball he's over there whining and we're all going to need ear plugs. No way!"

Determined, I stomped off. But Larry stopped me again, and this time he was dead serious.

"Okay knock it off, enough of this!" he demanded in a voice that immediately stopped me in my tracks. "I am your coach, and I tell you what to do. Is that clear?"

I looked over to my friends. No, it wasn't quite clear to us yet. This is not how we imagined our practice was going to be. Roger laughed his typical laugh. "Hey, guys, whatever. Yesterday we danced here. Why not play with a cute little fuzzy yellow ball today?"

"And what's on for tomorrow, a hard-boiled egg?" Danny laughed and we all chimed in. But today's laughter was not quite the same as yesterday. Perhaps this was because we were all sore and cranky. With that, we began our practice.

Larry divided us into two teams. Danny, Tyler, Roger, and me against Alex, Diego, Julian, and Josh. Then he tossed the tennis ball onto the field. Oh man, this was harder than it looked! We learned the day before how to move on the mushy field, but that tennis ball had not. It was hiding in clumps of grass as if it wanted to play below the turf. Then, if one of us had it, it slipped through our feet or bounced off our shoes straight to the other team. We barked at each other more and more:

"Watch out!"

"Where'd you learn how to play?"

"Loser!"

Larry stepped in every time. He didn't let us yell and insult each other. We were a team, he said, and everyone had to grow and learn together. But we were all irritated. And on top of that we were sore and Sox wouldn't stop howling and so, again and again, one of the *Wild Bunch* would get frustrated, sit down on the ground or yell at Larry.

"I've had it!"

"I'm not playing anymore."

"That's it, I quit."

But Larry stayed firm. He reminded us that we only had two weeks and our number one goal was to beat the *Unbeatables*. And that's why he tortured us with the tennis ball.

"If you succeed with the tennis ball," he promised again and again, "every trick with the soccer ball will feel like child's play."

We sucked that day. In the evening, the lemonade tasted bitter and we walked home with our tails between our legs. We were so depressed we didn't say a word, and every one of us thought to himself: "We'll never beat the *Unbeatables* if *this* keeps up."

"We're never going to get our soccer field back."

And: "Even if Larry is right, how can we possibly keep

going like this for the next ten days?"

The next three days were even worse. It got hot. As hot as the dog days of summer, and with the heat came the mosquitoes. They buzzed around us and bit our arms and legs and faces. And then there was Sox's howling, which wouldn't stop even when we took turns sitting next to him. He didn't like to be petted. He just wanted the ball. He was crazy for that thing, and the more he liked it, the more we hated it. We yelled at each other, cursed each other like crazy, and once I even grabbed Roger and pushed him into the mud.

"Moron! Start playing soccer for once!"

Larry tried to calm us down, but we hissed at him:

"Stay out of it!"

"This was your idea!"

"This is all your fault!"

"Let's see you try it. Let's see if you can do any better with that lame leg of yours."

Everyone shut up, including Larry, who limped to the sidelines and sat down and just watched us. At first we thought, "Hah! That'll show him! Now we'll stop playing!" But then we just stood there, looking at each other. We knew that whoever left first was a coward and no one wanted to admit to that. Nobody wanted to be the reason for losing the game. Nobody wanted to be the reason for losing our neighborhood soccer field. Ashamed, I walked to the ball, balanced it on the instep, lifted it up in the air, headed it, stopped it with the chest and, with my

knee, kicked it to Danny. He did the same, and passed it on to Alex. Next came Julian, then Tyler, then Diego. It didn't fall into the mud until Roger had it. But we didn't care. We were laughing again, and eventually we all got the big picture. We played like Kaka and Ronaldinho at the beach in Brazil. Larry had told us about them many times, but we must have forgotten. At the beach you play the ball high, because otherwise it'll just bounce around out of control. That's why the Brazilians are such magicians with the ball, and that's why we were magicians now, too — except Josh and Roger.

I didn't say anything for the next two days. Maybe that was because I had traded my ball for Sox. We didn't need the ball anyway and that way at least we didn't have to listen to Sox's howling. But then things started to annoy me. Every time Roger or Josh had the ball, they lost it and the other team scored a goal. The two of them were totally clumsy and to make things worse, they hadn't learned a thing. Okay, I admit it, Josh was still too young. He was only six years old, three years younger than me, so he's going to make mistakes, right? But Roger, though, he was just blind. Period. And then to top it off, Diego got sick. The fever finally caught up with him, and there were no more ice cubes to save him. His mother had defrosted the freezer.

That's why on the ninth day of our practice, four days before the game, I called a team meeting with Larry. And if you know me, you know I didn't hold my tongue.

"Josh and Roger have to leave the team!" I demanded. "Having them on our team is like having them on the other guys' team."

Josh and Roger were mortified. Josh jumped up and ran away and hid behind a tree and howled like Sox. But Roger stayed put and the others looked at me in silent scorn.

"What? You don't agree? You want them on the team?" I challenged, and when everyone remained silent, I pleaded to Larry.

"Come on, Larry, tell them what I mean."

But Larry just looked at me in dismay and shook his head.

"I only see a team. And the team you started with is the team you should finish with."

"Oh man, that's not what I meant. I want to win."

"Really?" Larry said. "Do you think you're the only one who wants to win?"

Larry glared at me, and the sheer power of his gaze silenced me. I knew then I was all alone in this. Not even Tyler was on my side. And I knew he hated to lose as much as I did.

"OK," I said, "fine. Then let's be honest. That's what you always say we should be, right?"

Larry nodded with his eyes, but I knew he wanted me to be quiet.

"OK," I said anyway. "Diego is sick. That means we only have seven players. Tell me honestly — are Roger and Josh soccer players?"

"Of course!" Larry answered. "They are playing the ball with their foot. That's what we call soccer around here." He smiled tentatively, and this smile asked me yet again to keep my big fat mouth shut. But I wiped the smile off his face.

"That doesn't answer my question. I want to know if you think they are good soccer players."

No one said a word. Not even Larry. He just shook his head.

"Say something, Larry," Roger said nervously. "You're our coach."

"What can I say?" Larry answered. "This isn't just about soccer. It's about friendship."

That scornful tone in his voice wasn't just for me. It included the others, too, because none of them tried to help Roger. So Roger got up, wiped the tears from his eyes, and walked away, slowly. Josh ran after him, and we watched until the two of them disappeared behind the trees.

"Nice going," Larry praised us. "Now you're down to five. Five super pros against seven unbeatable monsters. No doubt about it, on Saturday, victory will be yours."

The mocking in his eyes hit me square in the heart. I took a deep breath and then I said: "I agree. We're going to win." I met Larry's glare. "Give me one day and I promise: Tomorrow we'll be seven again."

Then I jumped up and ran off.

He Who Puts a Spell on the Ball

I ran and ran, until I was out of their sight. Then I stopped and took a deep breath. Oh man, why does everything have to be so hard! I sure didn't want to run into Roger and Josh right now. My guilty conscience stuck to me like gum on a shoe. The two of them used to be my friends, and that was over now, forever. For just a brief moment I wanted to turn around and undo everything, but then I shook the thought from my mind.

"But I am right!" I told myself. "I am!"

All I had done was say out loud what the others were thinking. They just didn't have the guts to say it. They were chicken. Everyone knew that with Roger and Josh on the team we'd lose and nobody would have forgiven them for that. Friendship aside, we definitely needed two new players, and I had already one of them in sight.

So I ran off. I ran until I came to Margate Park. From across the park I spotted him. He was there every day when I came home on the school bus. Every afternoon he played soccer with some other kids. And he was amazing.

This time, the boy was all alone. I saw some of the other kids on the field, ice cream cones in their hands, but he was sitting by the jungle gym, pulling out grass, moping.

"Hey, you!" I yelled, but he didn't hear me.

"Hey, you! Hey, you!" I yelled two more times. Then I approached him.

"Hey! Hello! Are you deaf, or something?" I asked and sat down next to him on the grass. But the boy didn't even look at me. For a moment I thought that maybe he really was deaf. Or maybe he was like Alex, and just didn't speak. I let out a sigh and gave it one last try.

"I get it. All the other kids went to get ice cream and your mom wouldn't let you go. What did you do?"

The boy pulled out more grass, this time with its roots.

"She sent me away," he said softly.

"What do you mean?" I had no idea what he was talking about. "Who sent you away?"

Finally the boy looked at me, and I could see that he was crying.

"My mother. She has a friend over."

"So?"

"So I'm stuck out here until they're done."

"Oh, I see," I acted as if I understood everything. "Done with what?" Clearly, I understood nothing.

"That's none of your business!" the boy said.

I shrugged my shoulders.

"OK, whatever. But that means you're available. You're not grounded are you?"

The boy looked at me with surprise and confusion.

I cleared it up for him: "You know, grounded. It's a common ailment with kids our age. Do you have the ailment?"

The boy grinned and shook his head.

"OK. So that means you can come along and practice with us. We have an important game on Saturday. A game that is about honor and pride."

"What kind of game?"

"A soccer game, what else? Do you think I play mini-golf?"

The boy burst out laughing.

"All right. Let's go then. Get changed!" I said and the boy ran off.

But after a few steps he stopped dead in his tracks.

"What will I wear?" Believe it or not, he actually said that.

"Your soccer gear, what else!" I answered.

"But this *is* my soccer gear."

I looked at his brown wool sweater, his checkered pants and down to his worn out sandals.

"Are you serious?" I asked.

"I don't have anything else," the boy said, and the smile vanished from his face. "Does this mean I can't play?"

"Excuse me? What?" I was completely confused. "What did you say?" I had stopped listening. I could only think of what I had seen from the school bus. My God! How could anyone play soccer so totally awesome in those totally tattered sandals?

"Can't I come with you?" the boy asked again.

I grinned at him. "Of course you're coming with me," I answered and hurried off. "I hope you don't mind your feet getting wet."

"I don't mind!" the boy said, now running alongside me.

"And a black eye?" I added gravely.

The boy stopped immediately.

"A black eye, what for?" He seemed to shiver with fear. "Listen carefully, I won't let anybody hit me!"

I swallowed hard. I didn't mean to scare him.

"Come on," I said in as normal a tone of voice as I could. "I'm just messing with you. I'll explain everything on the way, OK?"

He wasn't going for it and I didn't have much time. I had bitten off more than I could chew again. Where was I going to find a second player?

"OK," I sighed. "What's your name?"

"Joey," he said, still wary.

"I'm Kevin. And I'm sure you've heard of the *Wild Bunch*." Joey shook his head. I couldn't believe it.

"Dude! You can't be serious. The *Wild Bunch* are the guys who are going to kick Mickey the bulldozer and the *Unbeatables* to the moon."

"To the moon?" Joey asked, and his smile came back. "That's good. That's exactly where that jerk belongs."

"I'm with you!" I said. "And that's why we need to get going, now. We have to scour all the back yards in the neighborhood. We need one more guy, and I'll eat my knee

pads if there isn't at least one more boy in this hood who knows how to play soccer."

I hurried off, but Joey stayed put.

"Dude, now what?"

"You're just going the wrong way!" Joey grinned back. "Follow me," he said and walked to the hedge surrounding the trailer park and its playground. I was confused, but I followed him anyway.

Mr. Invincible

"Here," Joey said, "this is our guy."

He peeled aside the branches of huge hedge that separated the playground at Margate Park from the front lawn of a huge mansion.

"Who lives there?" I asked in amazement. "Landon Donovan?"

"No, more like Tim Howard!" Joey answered, pointing towards a corner of the huge lawn, where a nine-year-old boy was standing, kicking the ball against a wall and catching it with little effort.

"That's Kyle," Joey explained. "He plays with us once in a while."

"Great! You have some friends!" I was impressed and wanted to call out to Kyle, but Joey held me back.

"Wait. Not like that!" he said. "We have to be careful."

"Why?" I wanted to know. "Does he have a body guard who will beat us up if we set foot on the lawn?"

"No, not that bad. But close. Kyle is not allowed to play soccer, period."

"Oh, I get it, he's been banned from the sport. I know all about that. What did he do?"

"That's just it. He didn't do anything," Joey answered gravely. "It's his father. He thinks only boys like us play soccer. Um, I mean, boys like me. You know, boys who are total losers."

"Dude! That totally sucks!" I shook my head.

"Yeah, it sucks alright. He wants Kyle to be a golf pro. So no soccer."

"That's unbelievable," I sighed. "So, just because you live in a mansion doesn't mean you're hip to the greatest sport in the world. Now what do we do?"

Joey grinned at me.

"We'll use an old Shawnee trick. Do what you want, just don't get caught."

Joey put his hands to his mouth and squawked like an eagle. Immediately Kyle grabbed the ball, looked around to make sure nobody was watching, then ran towards us and slipped under the hedge.

"Hey, I thought you were spending the day with your mom today," he greeted us.

"Forget it," Joey answered. "I have something better."

"That's right!" I blurted out. "We're playing against Mickey the bulldozer and his *Unbeatables*. Are you in?"

"Does Beckham score from the halfway line?" Kyle laughed and together we ran off.

You can't imagine how surprised the others were when I showed up at the lake with Joey and Kyle. It took less than an hour, and the two new guys already showed off their skills. Roger and Josh were not only replaced in record time, they were completely forgotten. Our irritability disappeared and everyone was thrilled. But Larry wasn't happy. You could tell in his eyes, he was sad, but he coached us anyway, and he coached us well.

Then, after an excruciating workout, he finally he gave us a real ball. My ball. I had traded it in this morning for Sox. And when we finally felt the real ball at our feet after all those torturous days with the tennis ball, even Sox's howling didn't bother us.

We knew exactly what Larry had done for us these past few days. He turned us into real soccer players.

Almost everything worked, and two days before the game, Tyler stood up and lifted up his lemonade bottle.

"To Larry!" he said festively, "the best coach in the whole wide world!"

"Yes, to Larry, the best coach in the whole wide world!" we all shouted. And then, thunder roared from the sky and lightning flashed all around us. But we were not afraid; we felt free at last and ran through the rainstorm like a *Wild Bunch,* happily laughing.

The Best Soccer Players in the World

The next morning, the air was crisp and clear on the field by the lake. Larry even got Sox to stop howling. He put him with us.

"So," he said. "Although you crowned me 'best coach in the world' yesterday, that doesn't mean that you are the best soccer players in the world. Is that clear?"

"Wow, talk about supporting your team," I teased, but Larry looked me straight in the eyes.

"It would be nice if you practiced what you preached, Kevin. You make more mistakes than any of us."

"Bull," I hissed. "I can run circles around everyone and I score almost all the goals."

"Exactly. Because you never pass the ball to anyone else," Larry answered bluntly.

"Kiss my cleats!" I did not want to hear that kind of criticism. I knew that I was selfish, in love with the ball and stubborn, but that was just part of me. I was Kevin, the star striker and master dribbler, and that's precisely who I wanted to be. "You can try, but you'll never change me," I shot back.

"I don't have to," Larry smiled. "Sox will do that for me."

"Sox?" we all shouted with dread. "Enough talk about Sox. He's a total pain."

"Well, get ready for some *real* pain," Larry smiled, "I'm going to let him play against you. Or rather, you'll be playing against Sox. Sox will be in the center, and if you manage to pass the ball ten times before he grabs it, I'll call you the best soccer players in the world."

We looked at him in disbelief.

"That's not fair," Tyler said. "There's seven of us. Sox doesn't stand a chance."

"If that's true, today's practice should be over in no time," Larry was still smiling.

Then he tossed the ball and Sox raced after it. Tyler stopped the ball with his left foot in the air and moved it to his right for the pass. But Sox was faster and buried the ball underneath him.

"That wasn't fair," Tyler complained to Larry. "I couldn't stop the ball."

"OK, I'll make it easy on you," Larry suggested, took the ball away from Sox and gave it back to Tyler.

"Is this better?" he smiled again, and held Sox by his collar. Tyler nodded and prepared the ball for the pass. Then Larry let Sox go and the dog raced towards Tyler. He passed the ball just past Sox, and counted triumphantly: "One!"

But his pass was not as exact as it usually is and Julian had to hurry to get there before Sox. He stopped it with his heel, turned in a flash, and was about to count "Two!" but Sox was already there.

"That's not fair!" Julian yelled. "He's too fast!"

"Nonsense! You just have to trick him," I countered and took the ball.

Larry held Sox by the collar.

"Come on, let him go! I'm waiting," I ordered, and Sox came towards me. But this time he didn't run; he trotted slowly, his tail high up in the air, wagging.

"Come on, what are you waiting for?" I encouraged Sox. Then I faked the ball left, turned around lightning fast, and played the ball with my left heel to the right. Sox stopped and didn't do a thing the whole time. He shifted his head to the side and I was sure he thought I was completely

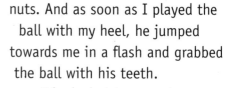

nuts. And as soon as I played the ball with my heel, he jumped towards me in a flash and grabbed the ball with his teeth.

I looked at Larry and surrendered.

"OK, you're right. We need work. *Now* what?"

Larry smiled again.

"Just pass, that's all," he said. "But be fast and precise."

We nodded and accepted our fate. Larry really was the best coach in the world, and more than anything we wanted to be the best players in the world. But two hours later, at noon, when the blazing sun burnt down on us, we only managed three lousy passes. The only one who was still on his game was Sox. He barked and wagged his tail and wanted more. But we needed a break. The lemonade evaporated in our throats and the only consolation we had was the knowledge that Mickey the bulldozer and his *Unbeatables* were even worse off.

The Bulldozer's Surprise Attack

The soccer field was like a ghost town and the *Unbeatables* were roasting in their own fat. Lifeless, they were lying scattered around Larry's stand, or rather, amidst the rubble of what was *left* of Larry's stand.

On the first day, as soon as Mickey the bulldozer understood that without Larry there was nothing to drink, he declared the stand a self-service counter. But the place was locked up tight as a drum. These losers didn't punch their fists through the walls or break the locks, they brought an ax and destroyed the place. But when they did it, they cut the electrical cords, and the refrigerators died. This turned the lemonade into sticky syrup, and when greedy Humungous tried to drink from one of the bottles, he almost choked.

Now, in the mid-day heat, they were helpless, and only two of them were still conscious enough to think.

One of the two was the Grim Reaper, and he looked at the other one, the Bulldozer, with worry.

"What do we do now?"

"Shut up!" the Bulldozer cursed. "We'll win tomorrow. That's all."

The Grim Reaper nodded, but his gaze wandered over to his lifeless team.

"I was just thinking..."

"Shut your trap!" the Bulldozer cut him off, and this time he threatened to hit him.

"Yeah but," the Grim Reaper dared to continue, "if this Larry guy is not here, doesn't that mean those snaps are really practicing?"

"Those snaps are lower than whale doo and that's two thousand feet below sea level," the Bulldozer snapped. "Now, shut up! I'm trying to think."

"Oh, right, sorry!" The Grim Reaper was impressed, and squirmed nervously.

"But even so, Mickey. This Larry fellow, I mean, he used to be a pro, right?"

He scratched his head and looked at the Bulldozer, carefully.

"And I mean, maybe he actually turned them into something. It really wouldn't be so good for you, Mickey, I mean for all of us, if we, uh, you know, lost tomorrow."

That's when Mickey hit him. His fist hit the Grim Reaper square in the nose. The Grim Reaper screamed and looked at Mickey, flabbergasted. "But Mickey, I just...!"

"But nothing," the Bulldozer barked at him. "Didn't I tell you to shut up, you moron? This Larry guy was never a pro. He played in a semi pro league years back, with my dad. Man, it was my dad who personally ruined the guy's knee!"

And with this memory, Mickey's face lit up.

"Come on! Get up already, you dork! I just had an idea."

Meanwhile, we were still training down by the lake, but we still hadn't managed to pass the ball ten times. Five passes at the most and it was over. Sox was just too fast and we were about to give up, when Larry suddenly got up and showed us a different side of him, a side we had never seen before. He danced around us like a goblin, ran alongside us, lame leg or no, encouraging us.

"Come on, Kevin, right. Pass to the right. Julian is free! Yes, that was good. That was number four! Yes, and Tyler, you have to go to the left. To the left, now you are free and, you see, that was number five! Yes, and now shoot it to Joey with your heel. Six! Man, you guys are good! And Joey, look, right there, it's Kyle in the middle. Come on, Kyle, run!"

But Kyle stood still, and Sox caught the ball. Embarrassed, Kyle looked at Larry, but Larry just applauded enthusiastically.

"Hey, man, that was a new record! You see? All you need to do is to keep moving, and Kyle, you need to move *towards* the ball. Approach it. Don't wait for it. Then Sox won't stand a chance! Come on, let's go. Next time you'll get it right, and then you won't only be the best soccer players around here, you'll be the best soccer team in the world!"

We were still skeptical, but Larry's enthusiasm was contagious. He danced around us again, and with his orders and tips the ball moved through our ranks like butter on a hot plate. We couldn't believe it when we reached number seven and number eight.

That's when Larry withdrew. He didn't say another word and sat down on the grass. But his eyes sparkled, that's how thrilled he was by our game.

We managed number nine and number ten and still kept playing. Sox ran between us, but it was all in vain. Finally, he yelped angrily and gave up at number seventeen. He stood in front of us, panting, barked one last time, then ran towards the tree, yelping. Then he lay down on his stomach and covered his eyes with his paws until I put

him on the leash. Sox was done with soccer for the day.
We ran towards each other, embraced each other, embraced
Larry, and then, for the first time, formed our circle.

Larry counted to three, and for the first time, without
any discussion, we yelled out what would become our
battle cry. All of us roared: "ONE, TWO, THREE WILD!"

But as soon as our battle cry had died away, a mocking
"woof" answered.

We whirled around. Sox had never barked that way.
That's because it wasn't Sox, it was Mickey the bulldozer.
We retreated a few steps until we realized that we were
already surrounded. We could see them approach from all
sides: Humungous, Mow-down, Juggernaut, Octopus, the
Grim Reaper, and Kong.

Sox growled at those morons. He sounded like a wolf
and was so convincing and wild that even Mickey the
bulldozer got nervous. He checked at least three times

that Sox was on the leash. Only then did he bark his "woof!" again and stopped in front of Larry.

"Pro, huh? And that's how you coach? Wow..."

Larry was embarrassed.

"I see. I almost thought this was a doggy school."

At his command, all the morons around us laughed. The Bulldozer turned away from Larry and approached us.

"Did he teach you just those tricks? I mean the great tricks you only know if you're a pro?"

We got mad.

"So what?" I spat. "What do you care?"

"Who, me?" Mickey asked, and lifted his arms as if he was innocence personified. "Oh, I don't care at all."

"So? Why are you here then?" I hissed. "Did you get lost?"

"Did you hear that?" The Bulldozer laughed. "You're that courageous twerp, aren't you?"

He leaned over me, his rasping breath was suffocating. "Don't worry, twerp. I won't do anything to you. *Today.* Today I mean you no harm. After all, tomorrow is our game and we want it to be really good. Am I right or am I right?"

"For once you're telling the truth," I spat.

"Exactly!" Mickey whispered into my face and I almost threw up. Then his voice was booming again.

"And that's why I'm here. To tell the truth. Just came to tell you your coach, Larry the Boozer, never was a pro. Am I right or am I right, lame leg?"

The question was addressed directly to Larry, but he kept quiet, and instead looked at us, embarrassed and unsure.

"Tell him, coach!" I yelled.

"Tell him it's a snappin' lie!" Danny demanded.

"You said it to all of us!" Tyler begged. And Julian encouraged him: "You are the best coach in the world!"

But Larry just looked at the ground, ashamed.

"What did I say?" Mickey the bulldozer roared. "Lame leg is one big lie. He told you a tall tale and — oh, I am so sorry — you tortured yourself for ten days straight, and all in vain. Or do I look like a dog?"

The morons laughed again at his command.

"Woof woof!" Mickey barked, and he laughed so loud that the fat underneath his Darth Vader shirt seemed to be dancing with the stars.

"Woof woof!" he barked again. "Which other animals did you pretend to be? Were you the crickets in the woods and the tadpoles in the puddles? Oh, snap! I'm going to die laughing! Ribbet, ribbet, ribbet!"

Mickey the bulldozer and his *Unbeatables* were shaking with laughter, and there was nothing we could do other than steel up and bear it. Finally, Mickey caught himself and wiped the tears from his face.

"Oh, never mind, twerps. Think of what I did for you as just a service between friends. I hope we'll still see you tomorrow morning at ten. And if not, then I know where I can find you. At the zoo. With the monkeys."

The Bulldozer screeched again with laughter and held onto his fat belly, making sure it didn't roll away. The other jerks joined in, then all of them wobbled away.

We stayed put and waited until they had vanished. Then we looked over at Larry.

"Is that true?" I asked.

Larry looked pitiful.

"Is that true?" I asked again.

"You know, I tried to tell you," he stammered.

"You said we should be honest!" Tyler reminded him.

Larry lowered his eyes.

"I know," he answered.

"And what are we supposed to believe now?" Julian asked.

"That we're going to beat the *Unbeatables?*" Danny mocked.

Larry looked at us. He pleaded: "You are the best soccer players in the world! You can believe that."

"And you are a liar, Larry," I stated. "We never want to see you again!" Larry turned away from us and rubbed his eyes. I think he was crying.

"Let's go!" I called out to the others. "There's nothing left for us here."

Without a word, we all walked past Larry and then headed home. It was over. We not only lost the soccer field, we lost all confidence in ourselves.

A Dark Night
and an Even Darker Morning

None of us slept that night. The same thoughts tortured us all. We were so disappointed. We worked so hard. We had given it our best. And we had believed in Larry. It was because of him we endured the muddy field, the tennis ball, the heat, the mosquitoes, and Sox's howling. For a brief moment we had reached the summit. We really believed we were the best soccer team in the world. But then Mickey the bulldozer showed up and shot us down. We fell thousands of feet into the abyss, and that's where we were now, defeated and lifeless. We were a joke, nothing but a laughing stock, and our confidence had been revealed as a cheap lie.

"But we beat Sox!" Tyler blurted out below me. It was probably three in the morning and he was still resisting the truth. You know, Tyler never gives up, and usually that's great. But in this case it just meant further torture.

Larry lied to us, and so, everything he taught us wasn't worth snap.

"But we beat Sox!" Tyler repeated at around three-thirty.

"So what!" I answered. "Did you forget what Mickey the Bulldozer does to dogs?"

"He pulls their ears off," Tyler said.

"Exactly!" I explained. "And that's why Mickey the bulldozer is not a dog. He's a monster. Have we beaten any monsters lately?"

There was no answer from Tyler this time.

"Tyler! Larry was never a pro, and we are not the best soccer team in the world."

"But we're still going to play the *Unbeatables*, right?" Tyler asked. He just couldn't leave it alone.

I just stared at the ceiling. Then I asked: "What's the point?"

At some point we must have fallen asleep, and in the morning even Tyler was so tired that he didn't want to get up. All of us tossed and turned all night. Our parents wanted to wake us, but we sent them away.

"The game has been cancelled," we said.

"Mickey the bulldozer broke his legs."

"Our ball is flat."

Then, at One Woodlawn Avenue, Alex opened his eyes. His father stood in his room, holding a brand new soccer ball in his hand. It was dark black.

"Nike," Alex's father said spinning the gleaming ball in his hands. "Limited Edition. There are only 5,000 of these babies in the world. I think it's just the right ball for a new collection."

Alex's father smiled at his son: "Assuming that you don't chicken out today." Then he was serious: "My son does not chicken out, am I right?"

He was. Alex jumped up and out of bed, grabbed the ball and stormed out of his room.

A few seconds later, Danny's mother stood at Danny's bed, handing him the phone.

"Hello? What's up?" Danny moaned into the phone but didn't get an answer.

"Dang it, Alex! What do you want from me? Oh no! Please don't tell me you want to play!"

Alex stood in his kitchen on the other end of the phone line, intently looking at his ball.

"Alex, you are nuts. There's no point to going out there," Danny said, but Alex just shook his head. He fought with himself and finally won. He said: "Yes, there is."

Danny flew out of bed.

"Dude! This is too much. Why did you have to choose a moment like this to start talking? Listen, I'm never going to forgive you! Oh, snap! Mom, where are my cleats?"

Five minutes later, a small pebble clicked against Julian and Josh's window in the house across the street. Josh jumped out of bed and looked outside. He saw Danny, Alex, Tyler, and me standing below. Josh panned his gaze over to his sleeping brother, thought about it, then yelled down into the street: "Sorry, but Julian can't come. He wet his pants when I told him you were playing."

In a nanosecond Julian was at the window, pushing Josh aside.

"That's a lie! I'm not afraid!" he yelled at us.

"Then what are you doing up there?" We grinned mischievously.

The five of us continued. It was already nine-thirty when we got to the trailer park to pick up Joey. But Joey's van was already gone and a neighbor told us Joey and his mother left in the middle of the night. Just up and left. That was a double-whammy, because now nobody knew how to imitate the eagle cry that would call Kyle. What would we do? Ringing the bell and asking for Kyle could mean the end of soccer for him. But if he was tossing and turning in his bed, he'd never find out that the game was on.

So I took heart, and even though the door was as big as a castle gate, I rang the doorbell. We waited forever and were about to leave, when suddenly somebody appeared. The guy holding a silver tray in his hand looked like a penguin.

"Oh, bonjour. May I 'elp you?" he asked.

We didn't understand a word: Why was this guy so polite? We were just kids. Adults aren't polite to kids.

"Edgar, who is it?" said a female voice with a nasal pitch. And then I saw another strange inhabitant of the house.

That inhabitant peeked out of a door behind the penguin, was stuck in a bathrobe and had a pound of lettuce on its face.

"Oh-la-la, you're 'ere to see zee lady of zee 'ouse?" Edgar asked us. " But ov course, zee newspaper interview. One moment please. Madame, zee gentlemen of zee 'erald are 'ere."

The bathrobe with the lettuce on its face shrieked in horror and slammed the door so hard that it shook the house. Horrified, we looked at the penguin.

"But, but we're not from the Herald," Tyler stammered.

"Shhh!" Edgar said and winked at us. "I 'ave a message for you. A zeecret message. It is top zeecret."

Again, we didn't know what he was saying.

"A message from junior. But first I need zee zeecret code." Edgar smiled.

"Dang, dude! What secret code and what junior are you talking about?" I asked and stomped my food impatiently. "We just want to see Kyle, that's all."

"I'm zorry, but vizout zee zeecret code I cannot tell you anyzeeng." Edgar was being difficult and looked just like a penguin again. "You are zee Vild Bunch, no? And you 'ave zees battle cry, no? Vat is it?"

"ONE, TWO, THREE WILD!" we yelled, and Edgar jumped a mile.

"Shhh! Not zo loud, it's zeecret, remember?"

"Well, then tell us already, penguin!" Danny urged, and Edgar looked at him with surprise.

"Penguin, oh-la-la! C'est bon!" he laughed. Then he leaned down to us. "'ere's the story, junior, I mean Kyle, 'ad to go play golf viz 'is father. But ve just called 'im.

As you can zee, Madame is at the end of 'er rope, and ve don't believe she can 'get zrough zee morning vizout zee monsieur."

He smiled at us, but we didn't understand a word.

"What is that supposed to mean?" I asked.

"Is Kyle on his way?" Danny asked. "Where is that golf club, anyway?"

"'alf an 'our from 'ere," Edgar answered and looked at his watch. "Oops, zat vill be very tight."

"You can say that again!" I hissed. It was quarter to ten already. "And you know what, penguin. I hate golf!"

Then we hurried off.

Be Wild!

Diego was waiting for us in front of the soccer field. Oh man, what a lucky break. At least there were six of us now.

"Hey man! Did you get over the flu?" I greeted him enthusiastically, but Diego, breathing heavily, shook his head.

"Then how did you get out?" Danny asked. "Did you ice a fly again?"

"No, I... I just took off!" Diego gasped, and that was when we realized he was having an asthma attack. But this one wasn't from the grass.

"What's wrong?" Tyler asked, worried now.

Diego just looked at him and pointed with his head to the soccer field.

We followed his gaze nervously and walked through the gate. For one split second we all thought we would have a group asthma attack, that's how lousy we felt. What was left of Larry's stand was strewn all over the ground, and the *Unbeatables* stood waiting behind it. They had torn their t-shirts and pants, and painted their faces. Then they roared:

"UAAAHH! UAAAHH!"

We stopped dead in terror. Now I knew for sure that I had been right. These guys were monsters, and what was ahead of us was no longer just a soccer game. I swallowed hard.

"Is Larry here yet?" I asked no one in particular.

"Larry? Are you kidding?" Mickey the bulldozer roared with laughter. "Larry has gone underground," he mumbled as if he was drunk, "if you know what I mean. Burp!"

We looked at the ground, ashamed. Mickey the bulldozer looked at his watch, gloating. It was ten sharp.

"Show time!" he rubbed his hands together. "Let the slaughter begin! What are you waiting for?"

"F-for Kyle," Diego gasped. "Seven aga-against six is not fair."

"Ohhhh!" the Bulldozer whined in response. "Quick! Call the wah-mbulance! Who ever told you life was fair?"

The morons all laughed at his command.

PHHHT

"And that's why we'll kick off and you'll play with the sun in your eyes."

Octopus, the Grim Reaper, and the others laughed again.

"That's how it is with duels. The one who's been challenged gets to choose the weapons."

Mickey the bulldozer placed the ball at the center mark.

"I suggest we play until one team has scored ten goals. That way I'll be back home in twenty minutes. I have plans later."

The Bulldozer searched his pockets and found a whistle. We still held back. We needed to play for time. We walked to our side of the field in slow motion, but the Bulldozer didn't wait. He blew the whistle and kicked the ball to the left. That's where Kong was waiting. We ran now, and I yelled orders to the others.

"I'll be goalie. Diego, play left. Danny, play right, and Julian, Alex, and Tyler, you stay back here with me."

But the others didn't hear me. They ran after Kong, who was almost as fast as Danny. That's why Mickey the bulldozer was free when Kong cross-passed. I ran out of the goal and threw myself into Mickey's shot. The ball thundered against my fists and I thought they'd break off. Still flying, I watched the ball roll over the goal line.

"One!" Mickey grinned, and I yelled at the others. "What kind of bull are you guys playing?"

But now we kicked off. We got ourselves into a line-up. Diego played to Danny, and Danny ran off. He ran as fast as he could straight at Humungous, Mow-down, and Juggernaut.

"Diego! Where are you?" he yelled. But Diego still stood at the center mark gasping for air. Danny had to go on by himself. He played the ball past Mow-down on the right, and ran around him on the left. Mow-down looked rather stupid, but Juggernaut came to his rescue and simply blocked Danny's way. Danny bumped into him full force, bounced off, and fell down. Juggernaut didn't even notice. He turned around, took the ball, and passed it to the Grim Reaper on the right.

Tyler attacked, but the Grim Reaper just pushed him to the ground.

"Hey! That was a foul!" I yelled, but Mickey the bulldozer just laughed.

"Body contact. Totally allowed."

Tyler was doubled up in pain, holding his ribs. Julian became all wild.

"OK. Body contact is totally allowed? You got it!" he yelled. At that very moment, the Grim Reaper passed to Mickey the bulldozer. Julian stormed towards him and tried to get to the ball first, but he ran straight into Mickey's elbow and it caught him in the right eye and he dropped to the turf like a sack of potatoes.

"Oh, my bad!" The Bulldozer grinned, turned and thundered the ball towards the goal so hard that I had to pull my fists away or lose them.

"Two!" Mickey's grin widened as he looked at his watch. "Two to nothing in one minute. Looks like I overestimated you."

I had enough. I grabbed the ball and ran to the center mark myself.

"Alex, you be goalie now," I yelled. "Diego, you pass to me."

Diego obeyed and kicked off. I took the ball and dribbled off. I played them dizzy, that's how mad I was. Humungous, Juggernaut, and Mow-down fell into the dirt behind me. That's when Danny and Tyler yelled: "Come on, Kevin, pass!"

But I was too angry. All I could see was Octopus, and behind him the *Unbeatables'* goal.

"Hey, Kevin! Pass!" Danny and Tyler yelled again. I saw them to my right and to my left, but I didn't even consider it.

That's when the Grim Reaper slid into my feet from behind and mowed me down.

"Foul!" I screamed and jumped up immediately.

"Is that so?" Octopus laughed, and grabbed the ball. "We call that playing the ball."

He stepped back to run and then kicked the ball high all the way across the field. That's where the Bulldozer was by himself against Julian and Alex. But Julian was no longer the Julian we knew. He did not only have a black eye, he was scared stiff. That's exactly what Larry said would happen. He wouldn't attack, and just a moment later Mickey the bulldozer lifted his arms and screamed: "Three!"

The *Unbeatables* laughed at us and ridiculed us as we trotted back to our end of the field, deflated. And then it got even worse. We started fighting: "See what happens if you do it all yourself?" Tyler criticized me.

"Leave me alone," I snapped.

"He's right!" Danny growled.

"Why don't you try it yourself!?" I barked.

Nothing worked, and although Alex stopped the next ball, we didn't stand a chance. After the next attack, Diego was wasted and plopped down at the edge of the field. Our legs were made of lead and we felt as if we were playing on the muddy field down by the lake. We forgot everything Larry had taught us, and we wished he were here. But there was no way he would come. I called him a liar. "I don't ever want to see you again," I said, and now it was five to zero in favor of the *Unbeatables*.

That's when I heard Mickey's mocking voice: "Halftime!" he said with a smirk, and gave us a break.

Roger the Hero!

We were too desperate and scared to notice we had two spectators. They had secretly followed us to the field. Now they were flat on their stomachs, hiding like Apaches on the warpath. They watched the game with bated breath through a hole in the fence, and when Mickey the bulldozer scored his first goal, one of them said to the other: "Tight! That's what they get."

After the second goal, the other one said to the first: "Excellent! Shoot 'em down."

And after the third goal, the first one even applauded enthusiastically. "Awesome! Don't stop now!"

But suddenly the second one jumped up and yelled: "No!"

Josh looked up, surprised, but Roger clenched his fists. "No! We didn't deserve that!"

"We?" Josh asked dumbfounded. "There's no 'we.' They kicked us out, remember?"

"Maybe, but I don't care. We didn't deserve that!" For a moment Roger burned a hole in the sky with his gaze. Then he ran off.

"I'm going to get Larry!" he yelled, and Josh watched him disappear.

"And what am I supposed to do?" he wanted to know.

"Get help!" Roger demanded, without stopping.

"Help?" Josh asked. "For who? For what?"

"Do I know?" Roger growled and kept running. "Just do it. We're going to need a superhero!"

Josh was at a loss, but shrugged and took off anyway.

Roger had no idea where he was going, he just ran and ran. He ran straight to the field by the lake. He had no idea why. But when he got there, he could already see him from afar.

"Larry!" he shouted. "Larry, we need you!"

But Larry didn't hear him. Roger ran over to him, but when he finally got there, all he could say was: "Snap!"

There were at least fifteen empty beer bottles on the ground surrounding Larry.

"You look like a fresh pile of you-know-what!" Roger mumbled. "Don't tell me you drank all that..."

Larry shook his head.

"I poured them all out," he said. "Apparently I tell too many tall tales when I drink."

"Can't argue with *that!*" Roger said, relieved. "If you're sober, let's go!"

"Go? Where?" Larry asked.

"To the soccer field, what do you think?!" Roger yelled, but Larry just shook his head.

"Dude! What's this crud?" Roger demanded to know. "Josh and I were kicked off the team too, but did we put our heads in the sand? I think not. No, we decided to show them just how valuable we really are."

"Good for you!" Larry smirked. "But they won't believe me anymore. I lied to them."

Roger smacked himself in the forehead.

"Oh man! So what? They *need* you. If you don't go now, the *Wild Soccer Bunch* is history."

Roger looked at Larry. Like a magnifying glass, his coke-bottle-thick glasses made his pleading eyes seem huge.

"Please, Larry," he tried one last time. "Do it for me. Those guys are my friends."

Larry turned around and looked out over the lake. Roger didn't see the tears in his eyes, and that's why he started yelling again. "Dang! Why didn't you just drink this stuff? If this is it, you should have just guzzled it all down!"

Roger wanted to run away, but he didn't know where to go. So he just sat down into the grass, behind Larry, staring at his back. He stared and stared at that back as if he wanted to hypnotize him, and suddenly, Larry actually got up.

"You're right!" he said. "Let's go." Before Roger realized what was happening, Larry took off.

Even Wilder!

Meanwhile, Joey paced up and down the EL train station like a caged tiger. He was way too late. All morning he had waited for his mother to wake up. She had promised she'd come with him to the game. But then she didn't come home until late that night with a strange man in tow. They were drinking and singing, and told Joey they were celebrating. But then they started fighting. And then his mother threw the strange man out of the van and took Joey in her arms instead.

"Forget that jerk!" she told him as she drove toward the highway. "Tomorrow I'll go meet your friends. They won't desert you, will they?"

"No," Joey answered, "but if you keep driving *I'll* desert them!"

That seemed to convince her. She stopped the van at the parking lot of a grocery store just off the highway and went to sleep. The next morning, she wouldn't wake up.

He waited until it was too late, then he woke her up. But she just yelled at him. So he wrote her a letter.

"Dear Mom," he wrote. "I love you."

He stepped out of the van and ran to the EL station,

and paced up and down until a train came that could take him to his destination. Then he ran to the soccer field, bumped into Kyle at the corner, and together, they hurried through the gate.

And they stopped. What they saw was worse than a knockout punch in the first round. Mickey the bulldozer stood in front of his *Unbeatables*, telling them with broad gestures and loud laughter how unbeatable they were. Five goals in just seven minutes, and all of them he had scored himself. He had not felt this good in ages. Behind him, we were down on the grass, staring at our feet. Julian's eye was darkgreenblueviolet, Tyler held his ribcage, and I licked my badly scraped knee.

Kyle and Joey sat down next to us in the grass.

"Not quite going the way we planned, is it?" Kyle joked carefully, but the only ones who thought it was funny were the *Unbeatables*. That's when Joey jumped up, fuming with anger.

"We'll see who has the last laugh."

Mickey the bulldozer exploded in laughter, holding his flabby belly. But then the laughter vanished from his face. His beady eyes glowed like lasers, shooting deadly glances above our heads. We turned around. Larry and Roger stood behind us. Larry's poker face hurled Mickey's lasers straight back at him.

"I think Joey is right!" Larry said, as if he was carving his words in stone. In that very instant, a cloud darkened the sun, and Mickey the bulldozer instinctively stepped back.

"Wow! Strong words," he tried to save face. "Did you hear that, guys? What are we waiting for? Let's finish them off!"

"Hold it! Just one minute!" Roger chimed in and took two steps forward. "On one condition."

Mickey the bulldozer raised his eyebrow.

"Condition?" he hissed.

"Yes, condition!" Roger held his gaze. Then he took a deep breath. "The team that loses fixes Larry's stand."

Mickey stared at him as if he wanted to kill him with his glare. But then his fat belly jiggled, made waves, and jiggled again, and then the Bulldozer snorted.

"Dude!" he laughed. "Hold on to that thought!"

The other morons joined in his laughter, and they walked to their side of the field, still snickering, when a battle cry cut into their laughter like a knife.

"ONE, TWO, THREE WILD!" we roared, standing shoulder to shoulder in a circle. Then we stormed apart. I kicked off, passed to Alex, who played back to Tyler, who in turn tendered a dream pass to the right, just in time to find Danny running up the sidelines. He played to me and I passed on to Joey to the left. The *Unbeatables* were watching us, paralyzed like flies caught in a web. Joey jumped over Mow-down's legs and passed back to me before Humungous could waddle over. I took a shot. The ball flew towards the high post. I was about to lift my arms in triumph when Octopus extended his tentacles and caught the ball effortlessly.

We sighed, and that woke the flies from their sleepy

paralysis. Octopus thundered his deadly goal kick towards Kong. Julian was right on him, but he was still scared. Kong left him in the dust and passed the ball to Mickey. The Bulldozer thundered at the goal, immediately. Kyle guessed the right corner. He flew, touched the ball with his fingertips and pushed it away. But unfortunately, he didn't push hard enough. The ball bounced against the inside goal post and from there right into the goal.

"Six!" The Bulldozer hollered and reached his arms towards the dark clouds.

We trotted back, beaten, looking for Larry. He applauded.

"That was great! Keep it up, men!"

"You're kidding!" I yelled at him. "We're losing, six to zero!"

Larry ordered me off the field.

"You want to have that attitude; you can sit on the bench."

He replaced me with Diego for the attack.

We attacked again, this time from the left. Joey passed to Diego, who passed to Danny, who took a shot at the goal. But the ball thundered against the post.

"Not fair!" I yelled.

"Yes, it is!" Larry countered. "You guys don't believe in yourselves. Don't you understand? Your opponents need to have respect for you. Tell that to Julian when you're going back in now. He needs to really rattle Kong and Mickey. I'm not talking about a foul, you hear? The *Unbeatables* are better at that. And you have to pass back to Alex. Let him score the goal. Do you hear me?"

I shook my head, but Larry smiled at me encouragingly. "Go on, get back on the field!"

The fact that the Bulldozer scored his seventh goal that very minute didn't seem to bother him one little bit.

This time we attacked through the middle. Tyler ran with the ball directly towards the goal. Mow-down and Juggernaut teamed up against him. Humungous came from the left. But Tyler didn't seem to mind at all. In the very last moment he passed to Danny on the right. He passed across the field towards the penalty spot. That's where I plucked the ball from the air and stood, free, in front of Octopus. He waved his tentacles. He seemed bigger than the goal. But my feet were still itching. I wanted to score. That's when I felt something behind me, and so I passed back with my heel. The Grim Reaper slid into me. I fell to the ground, but my pass had reached Alex with time to spare. And Alex the cannon thundered the ball toward the goal. Octopus threw himself into it, but when the ball hit his chest, he moaned and flew into the goal along with the ball.

I don't know who was more surprised, the *Unbeatables* or us. In any case, it took a while before we realized this was our first goal. It might have been seven to one, but to us, it was one to seven, and we ran into our half of the soccer field, cheering, getting ready for our opponent's attack.

Mickey the bulldozer grinned mockingly. Then he passed

to the side to Kong. He ran forward, stormed past Alex
and then further to Julian. But this time Julian did not
avoid him. He hit a press ball against Kong's foot. Kong,
surprised, sidestepped to the left, and stopped abruptly.
Julian stood in front of him again. Kong looked behind
him and to the right and couldn't believe what he saw.
Julian was everywhere, waiting. Julian Fort Knox, our all-
in-one defender, had come back to life. Before Kong even
knew what was happening, Julian had the ball, passed
it to Joey, who took the shot at the goal. Octopus flew
towards it, but because he was more careful after Alex's
cannon ball, he fisted the ball. The ball flew towards me
and I did my move, the famous "flip over bicycle kick."
Seven to two.

It started to rain when the score was seven to four.
The ground grew soft and muddy, and the *Unbeatables*

were sliding around like ducks on an ice rink. But we had practiced on that kind of field for twelve days, and so we were dancing through the ranks of our opponents. I scored my third goal, a real hat-trick; Danny his second; and then Joey pounded the ball directly in the corner to make it an even seven to seven. Tyler, our number 10, reigned in midfield and was rewarded with a shot from halfway down the field. The ball kept flying and flying until it was caught by a gust of wind, which carried it all the way to the goal where it sank, unreachable for Octopus' tentacles, directly into the goal. That was number eight. Now we were in the lead, and when Diego forgot all about this asthma and became the Tornado again, we scored number nine. We were lying in each other's arms and we knew we had won. That's when I lost the ball. I didn't pass. I wanted to score the tenth goal so badly. As a consequence, Larry took me off the field. He put Roger in instead.

"You can't be serious!" I yelled at Larry. "Do you want us to lose?"

Roger hesitated for a moment. He sure didn't want to be responsible for losing. He was about to leave the field and go back to the bench, but Larry yelled "Go on Roger, get on the field! Without you they'd have lost long ago!"

Then Mickey scored the *Unbeatables'* eighth goal and left them only one goal behind. It wasn't Roger's mistake, but when Roger missed the opportunity for the winning goal, I jumped up. I wanted to curse him, but Larry's glance kept me quiet.

Then the Grim Reaper evened the match. It was nine to nine, and the next goal would decide the game. I couldn't stand it any longer. I yelled at Larry: "OK, OK, I'll pass the ball."

But Larry was still waiting. Roger had another sure chance, and again he missed the ball. After that only a miracle by Kyle could stop the winning goal by the *Unbeatables*. He fisted the ball out of the lower left corner with a nosedive. But the ball was still in play. We held our breath and our hearts stopped. Kong took the follow-up shot at the goal while Kyle was still on the ground. Then Kyle bounced up, pushed himself off with both arms and legs at the same time, transformed into Kyle the Invincible, and at the last moment steered the ball around the post.

During the corner kick that followed, Julian bounced into the Grim Reaper and went down, injured. He had to leave the field, and Larry sent me in to replace him. But I didn't want that. I didn't want to play defense. I was Kevin, the forward, but Larry wouldn't discuss it.

So I did my best. Roger stumbled over the ball yet again, and then Kong came towards me. I swallowed hard. This guy was a real giant. But then I remembered what Julian would do in a situation like this. I approached him, slid right into him, hit the ball and jumped up. Then I ran. I ran and ran and dribbled around everyone who'd get in my way. I was Kevin, the master dribbler. And because I wanted to be the star striker on top of that, I didn't pass.

I ignored the calls from the others, until I stood right in front of the goal. Only Humungous and the Grim Reaper stood in my way. I grinned at them. I'd get around them, too. I didn't care that our goal was without any defense and that there was nobody covering the Bulldozer and Kong. I would handle this right here and right now. That's when I heard Roger. He ran behind me on the right. "Oh my God," I thought! "You messed up three times already." I played the ball past Humungous and wanted to play the ball through the Grim Reaper's legs. But Roger yelled again: "Watch it, Kevin, on your right!"

All I saw was the shadow. It was Mickey the Bulldozer himself. Like a crashing jumbo jet, he was sliding straight at me. That's when I passed the ball to the right, lightning fast. Roger ran towards the ball and took aim with the wrong foot.

"No, not with your left!" I yelled at him.

But Roger didn't listen. He was way too determined, and this time he actually hit the ball and thundered it into the net.

WE WIN!

We fell all over each other. Then we carried Roger on our shoulders and ran across the field with him. Only I was lying in front of the goal. I couldn't believe it that Roger the Hero had really become our hero. That's when Larry appeared before me and held out his hand.

"Congratulations!" he said.

"What for?" I barked up at him.

"For not just being Kevin, the master dribbler and star striker, but also for pulling off the most stubborn assist in the whole wide world."

He grinned at me and I grinned back. Then I took his hand. He pulled me up, and together we joined the others. Roger and I embraced each other, and shoulder to shoulder we continued our victory round.

"Great goal!" I said. "Thanks for not listening to me!"

"Great pass!" said Roger. "A Cristiano Ronaldo classic."

"Anyway, if you had not warned me of Mickey, then..." I couldn't finish the sentence.

"Then what?" hissed Mickey the bulldozer.

He stood directly in front of us, and behind him stood his beaten *Unbeatables*. They were fuming with anger, and they were ready for anything. In a heartbeat it was dead quiet. And in that quiet all you could hear was the bicycle chain the Grim Reaper had taken off his chest. He gave it to the Bulldozer who swung it, menacingly.

"The game was a joke," he said, showing his darkest grin. "You know that, don't you? I mean, I don't have to make myself any clearer?"

We looked at him. His beady eyes burnt holes into us. His breath rattled and the bicycle chain hit upon his hand rhythmically, like a ticking time bomb set to go off.

"I mean, you don't really think that the soccer field is yours now, do you?" he threatened.

Helpless, we retreated slowly. We had won, and lost anyway. That's when we heard a growl behind us. We turned around and saw Josh and Sox, who lifted his chops and showed his impressive teeth.

The Bulldozer's face twitched nervously.

"Who are you?" he barked, not so cool anymore.

"We're the superheroes," Josh laughed amused. That's when Sox charged ahead.

Mickey the bulldozer tightened the bicycle chain between his hands, but just to be safe, he took two steps back.

"I'm warning you!" he threatened us. "Get your dog. You know what I'll do with him, if you don't."

But Sox charged at him with a growl. He looked like a wolf. Actually, Sox's ears are so big that he looks more like a bat. But when he's angry and bares his teeth, the bat ears are not so noticeable any more.

"I'm warning you!" Mickey the bulldozer yelled again. Then he thought it best to run.

"Go, Sox! Tear his ears off!" we called after him.

"You'll pay for this!" Mickey called back at us as he retreated over the wooden fence. The other nitwits ran and jumped after him. They vanished exactly the way they had appeared: The way cockroaches do when you turn on the light.

We had a fantastic time in store for us. Sox was proudly wagging his tail and Roger and I were friends again. The sun broke through the dark clouds, opening the sky far and wide, all the way to the horizon.

THE END OF BOOK ONE!

JOACHIM MASANNEK
Born in 1960. Studied
German and Philosophy in
college. He also studied
at the University of Film
and Television; worked
as a camera operator, set
designer, and screenwriter
in films and TV.

His children's book
series *The Wild Soccer
Bunch* has been published
in 28 countries. As the
screenwriter and director
of the five *The Wild Soccer
Bunch* movies, Joachim
has managed to bring
about nine million viewers
into the theatres. He
was the coach of the real
Wild Bunch soccer team,
coaching his sons Marlon
and Leon.

JAN BIRCK
Born in 1963. Illustrator,
animation artist, art
director (advertising,
animation, CD-ROM's),
cartoonist, and CD-ROM
designer. Jan designs
The Wild Soccer Bunch
merchandising with
Joachim. Jan lives in
Munich with his wife
Mumi and his soccer
playing sons Timo
and Finn.

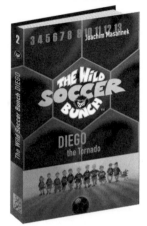

THE WILD SOCCER BUNCH
BOOK 2
DIEGO the Tornado

Fabio, the son of a famous Brazilian soccer player for the Chicago Fire, joins Diego's class. Diego envies the new kid when the rest of the *Wild Bunch* welcomes him with open arms. But Fabio's father has other plans. He thinks his son should play for a real club team, not for some street urchins, and signs him up to play with the Chicago Fire Youth Club.

Diego and the rest of the *Wild Soccer Bunch* are devastated, but instead of taking it lying down, they decide to become a real club team! They draft rules and create a team jersey, complete with *Wild Soccer Bunch* logo, and practice as a real club team.

Now the real test: challenge none other than the Chicago Fire Youth Team!

Can their friendship survive the challenge?

And can the *Wild Soccer Bunch* survive the game?

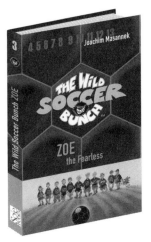

THE WILD SOCCER BUNCH
BOOK 3
ZOE the Fearless

Zoe is ten and soccer-crazy. She spends each day dreaming of becoming the first woman to play for the U.S. Men's National Soccer Team. Her dad believes in her dream, and encourages her to join the *Wild Soccer Bunch*. Even though Zoe would be the only girl on the team, she knows she could be their best player. But the *Wild Bunch* is not open-minded when it comes to welcoming new teammates, especially when they are girls...

Zoe's dad has a plan. He organizes a birthday tournament and invites the *Wild Bunch*. They present Zoe with a pair of red high heels, expecting her to make a fool of herself during the tournament. Zoe gladly accepts her gift. She wears the heels during the biggest game of her life, and proves that she's got what it takes to be a wild, winning member of the *Wild Soccer Bunch*.